Caught red-h.

I walked toward the door. At the same moment there was a crash of breaking glass. A bell went off. I turned and looked back.

It was impossible. A minute ago I'd been looking at a glass-topped cabinet with twelve red carbuncles inside. Now I was looking at a shattered cabinet with only eleven carbuncles lying in the wreckage. But apart from the security guards, there was nobody in the room. Someone had just stolen part of the Woburn windfall. The alarm bell was still ringing. But I knew it wasn't me and it couldn't have been them, so . . .

"All right, sonny. Stay where you are . . . Give it back, son," the security guard muttered, holding out one hand. He was moving very slowly, like I was dangerous or something. "You can't get away with it."

"Get away with what?" I squeaked. My voice seemed to have climbed up my nose and hidden behind my eyes.

I pushed my hands into my pockets. I wanted to show them that they were empty, that it was all a terrible mistake. But before I could say another word, my palm came into contact with something cold and round. I took it out. It glittered in the sunlight.

BOOKS BY ANTHONY HOROWITZ

THE ALEX RIDER ADVENTURES:
Stormbreaker
Point Blank
Skeleton Key
Eagle Strike

THE DIAMOND BROTHERS MYSTERIES:
Public Enemy Number Two
The Falcon's Malteser

Public Enemy Number Two

A Diamond Brothers Mystery

ANTHONY HOROWITZ

PUFFIN BOOKS

PUFFIN BOOKS
Published by Penguin Group
Penguin Young Readers Group,
345 Hudson Street, New York, New York 10014, U.S.A.
Penguin Books Ltd, 80 Strand, London WC2R ORL, England
Penguin Books Australia Ltd, 250 Camberwell Road, Camberwell, Victoria 3124, Australia
Penguin Books Canada Ltd, 10 Alcorn Avenue, Toronto, Ontario, Canada M4V 3B2
Penguin Books (NZ), cnr Airborne and Rosedale Roads, Albany, Auckland 1310, New Zealand

Published in Great Britain by Walker Books Ltd, 1997, 2002
Published simultaneously in the United States of America by Philomel Books
and Puffin Books, divisions of Penguin Young Readers Group, 2004

5 7 9 10 8 6 4

Copyright © Anthony Horowitz, 1987, 1997

All rights reserved

Puffin Books ISBN 0-14-240218-4

Printed in the United States of America

Except in the United States of America, this book is sold subject to the condition that
it shall not, by way of trade or otherwise, be lent, re-sold, hired out, or otherwise
circulated without the publisher's prior consent in any form of binding or cover
other than that in which it is published and without a similar condition
including this condition being imposed on the subsequent purchaser.

CONTENTS

FRENCH DICTATION

I didn't like Peregrine Palis from the start. It's a strange thing about French teachers. From my experience they all have either dandruff, bad breath, or silly names. Well, Mr. Palis had all three, and when you add to that the fact that he was on the short side, with a potbelly, a hearing aid, and hair on his neck, you'll agree that he'd never win a Mr. Universe contest . . . or a *Combat Monsieur Univers* as he might say.

He'd only been teaching at the school for three months— if you can call his brand of bullying and sarcasm teaching. Personally I've learned more from a stick of French bread. I remember the first day he strutted into the classroom. He never walked. He moved his legs like he'd forgotten they were attached to his waist. His feet came first, with the rest of his body trying to catch up. Anyway, he wrote his name on the blackboard—just the last bit.

"My name is Palis," he said. "Pronounced 'pallee.' P-A-L-I-S."

We all knew at once that we'd gotten a bad one. He hadn't been in the place thirty seconds and already he'd written his name, pronounced it, and spelled it out. The next thing he'd be having it embroidered on our uniforms. From that moment on, things got steadily worse. He'd treat the smallest mistake like a personal insult. If you spelled something wrong, he'd make you write it out fifty times. If you mispronounced a word, he'd say you were torturing the language. Then he'd torture you. Twisted ears were his specialty. What can I say? French genders were a nightmare. French tenses have never been more tense. After a few months of Mr. Palis, I couldn't even look at French doors without breaking into tears.

Things came to a head as far as I was concerned one Tuesday afternoon in the summer term. We were being given dictation and I leaned over and whispered something to a friend. It wasn't anything very witty. I just wanted to know if to give a French dictation you really had to be a French dictator. The trouble was, the friend laughcd. Worse still, Mr. Palis heard him. His head snapped around so fast that his hearing aid nearly fell out. And somehow his eyes fell on me.

"Yes, Simple?" he said.

"I'm sorry, sir?" I asked with an innocent smile.

"Is there something I should know about? Something to give us all a good laugh?" By now he had strutted forward and my left ear was firmly wedged between his thumb and finger. "And what is the French for 'to laugh'?"

"I don't know, sir." I winced.

"It is *rire*. An irregular verb. *Je ris, tu ris, il rit* . . . I think you had better stay behind after school, Simple. And since you seem to like to laugh so much, you can write out for me the infinitive, participles, present indicative, past historic, future, and present subjunctive tenses of *rire*. Is that under-stood?"

"But, sir . . ."

"Are you arguing?"

"No, sir."

Nobody argued with Mr. Palis. Not unless you wanted to spend the rest of the day writing out the infinitive, participles, and all the restiples of the French verb *argumenter*.

So that was how I found myself on a sunny afternoon sit-ting in an empty classroom in an empty school struggling with the complexities of the last verb I felt like using. There was a clock ticking above the door. By four-fifteen I'd only gotten as far as the future. It looked as if my own future wasn't go-ing to be that great. Then the door opened and Boyle and Snape walked in.

They were the last two people I'd expected to see. They were the last two people I *wanted* to see: Chief Inspector Snape of Scotland Yard and his very unlovely assistant Boyle. Snape was a great lump of a man who always looked as if he was going to burst out of his clothes, like the Incredible Hulk. He had pink skin and narrow eyes. Put a pig in a suit and you wouldn't be able to tell the difference until one of them went oink. Boyle was just like I remembered him: black hair—permed on his head, growing wild on his chest. Built like a boxer and I'm not sure if I mean the fighter or the dog. Boyle loved violence. And he hated me. I was only thirteen years old and he seemed to have made it his ambition to make sure that I wouldn't reach fourteen.

"Well, well, well," Snape muttered. "It seems we meet again."

"Pinch me," I said. "I must be dreaming."

Boyle's eyes lit up. "I'll pinch you!" He started toward me.

"Not now, Boyle!" Snape snapped.

"But he said—"

"It was a figure of speech."

Boyle scratched his head as he tried to figure it out. Snape sat on a desk and picked up an exercise book. "What's this?" he asked.

"It's French," I said.

"Yeah? Well, it's all Greek to me." He threw it aside and lit a cigarette. "So how are you keeping?" he asked.

"What are you doing here?" I replied. I had a feeling that they hadn't come to inquire about my health. The only inquiries those two ever made were the sort that people were helping them with.

"We came to see you," Snape said.

"Okay. Well, you've seen me now. So if you don't mind . . ." I reached for my book bag.

"Not so fast, laddie. Not so fast." Snape flicked ash into an inkwell. "The fact is, Boyle and me, we were wondering . . . we need your help."

"My help?"

Snape bit his lip. I could see he didn't like asking me. And

I could understand it. I was just a kid and he was a big shot in Scotland Yard. It hurt his professional pride. Boyle leaned against the wall and scowled. He would rather be hurting me.

"Have you heard of Johnny Powers?" Snape asked.

I shook my head. "Should I have?"

"He was in the papers last April. The front page. He'd just been sent down. He got fifteen years."

"That's too bad."

"Sure, especially as he was only fifteen years old." Snape blew out smoke. "The press called him Public Enemy Number One—and for once they were right. Johnny Powers started young . . ."

"How young?"

"He burned down his kindergarten. He committed his first armed robbery when he was eight years old. Got away with four crates of Mars bars and a barrel of Gatorade. By the time he was thirteen he was the leader of one of the most dangerous gangs in London. They were called the Slingshot Kids . . . which was quite a joke as they were using sawed-off shotguns. Johnny Powers was so crooked he even stole the saw."

There was a long silence.

"What's this got to do with me?" I asked.

"We got Powers last year," Snape went on. "Caught him red-handed trying to steal a million dollars' worth of designer clothes. When Johnny went shoplifting, you were lucky if you were left with the shop."

"So you've got him," I said. "What else do you want?"

"We want the man he was going to sell the clothes to."
Snape plunged his cigarette into the inkwell. There was a dull
hiss . . . but that might have been Boyle. "The Fence," he went
on. "The man who buys and distributes all the stolen prop-
erty in England . . . and in most of Europe, too.

"You see, Nick, crime is big business. Robberies, burgla-
ries, hijacks, heists . . . every year a mountain of stuff goes
missing. Silver candlesticks. Scotch whiskey. Japanese
stereos. You name it, somebody's stolen it. And recently we've
become aware that one man has set up an operation, a fantastic network to handle it—buying and selling."

"You mean . . . like a shopkeeper?"

"That's just it. He could be a shopkeeper. He could be a
banker. He could be anyone. He doesn't get his hands dirty
himself, but he's got links with every gang this side of the
Atlantic. If we could get our hands on him, it would be a disaster for the underworld. And think of what he could tell us!
But he's an invisible man. We don't know what he looks like.
We don't know where he lives. To us he's just the Fence. And
we want him."

"We want him," Boyle repeated.

"I think I get the general idea, Boyle," I said. I turned
back to Snape. "So why don't you ask this Johnny Powers?"
I asked.

Snape lit another cigarette. "We have asked him," he
replied. "We offered to cut his sentence in half in return for
a name. But Powers is crazy. He refused."

"Honor among thieves," I muttered.

"Forget that," Snape said. "Powers would sell his own grandmother if it suited him. In fact he did sell her. She's now working in an Arabian salt mine. But he wouldn't sell her to a policeman. He hates policemen. He wouldn't tell us anything. On the other hand, he might just slip the name to someone he knew. Someone he was friendly with . . ."

"What are you getting at?" I asked. I was beginning to feel uneasy.

"Johnny Powers is fifteen," Snape went on. "Too young for prison—but too dangerous for reform school. So he was sent to a special maximum-security center just outside London— Strangeday Hall. It's for young offenders. No one there is over eighteen. But they're all hardened criminals. We want you to go there."

"Wait a minute . . . !" I swallowed. "I'm not a criminal. I'm not even hardened. I'm a softy. I like cuddly toys. I'm—"

"We'll give you a new name," Snape cut in. "A new identity. You'll share a cell with Powers. And as soon as you've found out what we want to know, we'll have you out of there. You'll be back at school before you even know it."

Out of one prison into another, I thought. But even if I could have skipped the whole term, I wouldn't have considered the offer. Snape might call Powers crazy, but that was the craziest thing I'd ever heard.

"Let me get this straight," I said. "You want to lock me up with some underage Al Capone in a maximum-security jail somewhere outside London. I'm to get friendly with him, preferably before I get my throat cut. And I'm to find out who this Fence is so you can arrest him, too."

"That's right." Snape smiled. "So what do you say?"

"Forget it! Absolutely not! You must be out of your mind, Snape! Not for a million bucks!"

"Can I take that as a no?" Snape asked.

I grabbed my bag and stood up. Mr. Palis and his irregular verbs could wait. I just wanted to get out of there. But at the same time Boyle lurched forward, blocking the way to the door. The look on his face could have blocked a drain.

"Let me persuade him, Chief," he said.

"No, Boyle . . ."

"But—"

"He's decided."

Snape swung himself off the desk. Boyle looked like he was going to explode, but he didn't try to stop me as I reached for the door handle.

"Give me a call if you change your mind," Snape muttered.

"Don't wait up for it," I said.

I left the two of them there and walked home. I didn't think I'd hear from them again. I mean, I'd told them what I thought of their crazy idea—and they could always find some other kid. The way I figured it was, they'd just forget about me and go and look for somebody else.

Which just shows you how much I knew.

THE PURPLE PEACOCK

It was teatime when I got back. But that's not a great time when you can't afford the tea.

I was still living with my big brother Herbert—although that's not what he calls himself. He was born Herbert Simple but he changed his name to Tim Diamond and that's what it said on the door—

TIM DIAMOND INC.
PRIVATE DETECTIVE

We were still paying for the paint. Tim had only ever successfully solved one case and it was me who had done all the work. That had brought in a bit of cash, but we'd spent most of it on a skiing holiday and medical bills for Tim's broken leg. We'd have claimed some health-insurance money, but it was someone else's leg he broke. The rest of the money had gone on new furniture and carpets for the flat. And now, as they say, we were flat broke.

Tea that day turned out to be beans on toast. We'd had beans on toast on Saturday and on Sunday, too. On Monday I'd complained, so Tim had served toast on beans . . . just for a change. There were still sixteen cans of beans left in the larder. What worried me was what we were going to do when we ran out of toast, although the way the bread was looking—curling at the edges and slightly green—it was more likely the toast would run out on us.

There were two letters waiting for me in the hall. One was a card from the local library—an overdue book. It was three months overdue and now it would cost me more to pay the fine than it would have to buy the book in the first place. It was called *How to Make Money in Your Spare Time.* Obviously it hadn't worked. The second letter was postmarked Australia. I could hear Tim whistling in the kitchen. He was about as musical as the kettle. I took the letter to my bedroom, threw my bag onto the floor and myself onto the bed. Then I read it.

Dearest Nicky [it began],

Just a quick note as Daddy and me are off to another barbecue. It's being given by someone who works with Daddy, selling doors. We've just had three more doors fitted in my bedroom, which is a bit peculiar, as they don't lead anywhere. But you know your father. He adores doors.

I hope you are well. I miss you very much and wish you were here with us. I'm sure you'd like Australia. The sun shines all the time (except at night) and there are lots of friendly people. Are you remembering to change your underpants once a week? I am sending you three pairs of Australian underpants in the next mail. Just be sure you don't put them on upside down!

I wish I could come and visit you and Herbert, but I'm very busy with the new baby. We've decided to call her Dora.
  Keep well,
  Love, Mumsy

I felt sorry for Dora. If she could have seen what lay ahead of her, she'd have probably toddled back to the orphanage. It's not that there was anything wrong with my parents. But you know how it is. Brush your hair. Clean your teeth. Don't slouch. Don't talk with your mouth full. There were more rules and regulations in my life than the highway code and I couldn't even cough without reference to paragraph three, subsection five of the Bringing Up Children Act. When my parents emigrated to Australia, I slipped away to live with Tim. It wasn't much of a choice.

I threw the letter into a drawer and went into the kitchen. Even as I opened the door I realized there was a strange smell in the flat. Any smell that wasn't baked beans would have been strange, but this . . . ? Either I was going mad (from hunger) or this was fried onions.

Tim was standing by the stove wearing a pink apron, stirring something in a pan. I glanced at the table. There were two bulging shopping bags spilling out the sort of stuff I'd have dreamed about if I hadn't been too hungry to sleep. Biscuits, cakes, sausages, eggs, apples, and oranges . . .

"What's happened?" I asked. "No . . . let me guess. You

won a raffle? The Salvation Army called? You got a govern-
ment grant?" I snatched up an apple. "It's a miracle."

"No, it isn't," Tim said indignantly. "I got a job."

"That *is* a miracle. You mean . . . somebody paid you?"

"As of today I'm officially employed—in pursuit of the
Purple Peacock." Tim turned back to the frying pan. "How
do you want your steak? he asked. "Rare, medium, or well
done?"

"Large," I said.

Ten minutes later we sat down and ate the equivalent of
a week's worth of suppers rolled into one. There are times
when I'm genuinely fond of my big, blue-eyed brother. All
right, so he couldn't solve a crossword puzzle let alone a
crime. He had trouble tying his own shoelaces and he was
afraid of the dark. But we'd lived together for three years now
and things could have been a lot worse. They were about to
get a lot worse, as a matter of fact—but of course I didn't
know that then.

"What's the news from Australia?" he asked over the
chocolate mousse.

"Nothing much," I said.

"Did Mum send you any money?"

"No. But she's going to send me some underpants."

"Underpants!" Tim shook his head. "That's an affront."

"Actually it's a Y-front." I finished my pudding and threw
down the spoon. "All right, Tim," I said. "What's all this
about the Purple Peacock?"

THE PURPLE PEACOCK   13

"I've got to find it," Tim explained. "It's missing."

"From a zoo?"

"From a museum." Tim smiled. "It's not a bird. It's a vase."

He pushed the plates to one side and took out a notebook. His eyes had narrowed and his mouth was stretched tightly. This was the way he looked when he was trying to be a private detective. I don't know who he thought he was kidding. Not this kid anyway.

"It's a Ming vase," he went on. "Twelve inches high, blue and white, with a purple peacock enameled on the side." He flipped the notebook open. "It's fifteenth century. Made for the Emperor Cheng Hua."

"Cheng who?" I asked.

"No. Cheng Hua." He leaned back in his chair, spilling Coke down his shirt. "It's worth a mint—and I'm not talking Certs. There's only one vase like it in the world. It's worth thousands. For the last seventy years it's been on display in the British Museum. Then, a week ago, they sent it to be cleaned. Only it never got there. It went into the van at nine thirty-five A.M. exactly."

"And when the van arrived . . ."

"The van never arrived. It vanished, too. The driver stopped at a gas station in Camden. He went in to pay for the gas. When he got back to the pump, the van was gone."

"With the vase inside."

"That's right."

"So why hasn't the museum gone to the police?" I asked. "Why come to you?"

"They're too embarrassed to go to the police, Nick. I mean, that Ming was priceless. The museum wants it. But they don't want a scandal." He gave me a lopsided smile. "I'm the right man for the job. If they want to find their priceless vase, I'll crack it."

"You probably will," I said.

Tim poured himself another Coke.

"How much did they pay you?" I asked.

The smile returned to his face. "Two hundred in advance," he said. "Plus fifty a day in expenses."

"Fifty bucks!"

Tim shrugged. "I have expensive expenses."

"That's great." Even as I said it, my mind was ticking over. But I wasn't thinking about vases.

There was about to be a school trip to Woburn Abbey, the stately home and wildlife park. Now, I'm not exactly into stately homes—old suits of armor and dry, dusty paintings by dry, dusty painters—but the park sounded like fun, hurling stale doughnuts at the lions and getting a few laughs from the giraffes. The only problem was, we were expected to contribute to the cost: three dollars a head. I'd already missed out on Hampton Court and the Greenwich Observatory and the class was beginning to look on me as a charity case. They'd even passed a hat around for me. Not that I needed a hat, but it's the thought that counts.

"Tim," I muttered.

"Yes?"

"Since you've got a bit of cash now, do you think you could lend me a fiver?"

"A fiver?"

"You know . . . for Woburn Abbey. The school trip . . ."

He considered for a moment. "All right," he sighed. "But you do the washing-up."

He threw a crumpled five-dollar bill onto the table. I snatched it up. It had been so long since I'd seen a five-dollar bill, I'd even forgotten what color it was.

"Thanks a bunch," I said, wishing he had given me a whole bunch. I tucked the fiver into my shirt pocket. "So when do you start looking for the Purple Peacock?" I asked.

"Tomorrow." Tim lifted his glass. "I reckon I'll go back to the gas station in Camden. Find the pump assistant."

"And then?"

"I'll pump her."

He threw back the Coke in one. I think it was meant to be a dramatic gesture, but it must have gone the wrong way because his face went bright red and a second later he made a dramatic dash for the bathroom.

I watched him go. In all the excitement I'd forgotten to tell him about Snape and Boyle. But in truth I'd more or less forgotten about them myself.

WOBURN ABBEY

So that was how I found myself, a few days later, beetling up the M1 highway at fifty miles an hour on the way to Woburn Abbey. There were forty of us in the coach—thirty-eight pupils and two teachers. My friend Monsieur Palis was one of them. The other was an old guy, Mr. Roberts. He had been teaching history for so long that I reckon he must have been alive when most of it was going on.

We'd all been given packed lunches, which we'd unpacked and eaten before we'd even hit the motorway. Now the bus was strewn with potato chips, candy wrappers, and crusts of Mother's Pride. The driver couldn't have looked more miserable if he'd been driving a hearse. I'd managed to grab a place in the back row and we were all making faces at the other motorists to see who could be the first to cause a multiple pileup. Woburn Abbey was about an hour from London. Mr. Roberts had spent the first fifteen minutes giving us an abridged history of the place, which Palis had then translated into French. Nobody had listened. The sun was shining. If we'd wanted a history lesson, we'd have stayed at school.

At last we turned off the M1, and after rattling down a few country lanes and doubtless flattening a few country hedgehogs, we reached the grounds of the abbey itself. There was a sign pointing one way to the stately home and another to the safari park. Naturally we followed the first. I shifted on my seat and felt something jutting into my leg. Somebody had left a slingshot—a cheap, plastic thing wedged in the side of the chair. Without really thinking, I pocketed it. And that was all I had on me when we finally arrived: that and a couple of dollars in change from Tim's fiver.

The coach reached the parking lot and rumbled to a halt. We were all about to rush for the door, but then Palis stood up, raising a hand.

"Gentlemen . . ." he began.

I looked around me. I could see thirty-eight hooligans, but certainly no gentlemen.

"May I remind you," he went on, "that this is an historic outing. Woburn Abbey is a stately home, not an amusement arcade. In fact, the Marquess and Marchioness of Tavistock are still in residence here. So if there is any misbehavior, any tomfoolery, I shall deal with the matter personally."

His hand lashed out, sending a boy called Sington in a backward somersault down the aisle.

"And no chewing gum during the tour," Palis added with a twitch of a smile.

We trooped out more sheepishly after that. Even old Roberts seemed afraid of Palis. Two by two we marched down a winding path, past the restaurant, and through the turnstile. There was a sign up beside the ticket booth.

SPECIAL EXHIBITION
THE WOBURN CARBUNCLES
ON DISPLAY IN THE STATE SALON

"Please, sir," somebody asked. "What's a carbuncle?"

"It's a type of jewel," Mr. Roberts whispered, glancing nervously at Palis. "Quite a large jewel. It's normally red and—"

"No talking!" Palis snapped.

Mr. Roberts whimpered. Sington gave a strangled cough as he tried to dislodge the chewing gum from the back of his throat. Palis strutted forward.

We really were having a lot of fun.

I'm probably not the best person to describe a stately home. See one and you've seen them all as far as I'm concerned, and I wouldn't exactly get into a state if I didn't see any. I mean, tapestries and paintings and chandeliers and fancy tables are fine if you like that sort of thing in your front room. But just following a red rope around the place gawping at them . . . well, it's not my cup of tea—even if the cup is over three hundred years old and was once used by King Charles the First.

So I was bored by the book room, sent to sleep by the staircase, and I was hardly drawn to the drawing room either. You wouldn't believe how much stuff there was in that place. Paintings, mirrors, bronze clocks—you name it, at some time or other they'd bought it. By the time we got to Queen Victoria's bedroom, I'd have gladly thrown myself into the bed, even if the old girl had been in it at the time.

Our progress through the house had been watched by a number of antique ladies sitting in equally antique chairs. They were the only security on view and they looked about as lethal as a box of after-dinner mints. Half of them were knitting. The other half were smiling sweetly and blinking behind their horn-rimmed spectacles. But as we shuffled toward the Grand Salon, I noticed two security guards in uniform standing beside the door. One of them brushed against me as I went through. He didn't apologize.

The Grand Salon was like any other room in the house. Which is to say, it was certainly grand. This one was furnished in blue with blue chairs and sofas and blue murals on the walls. But the reason for the security guards wasn't blue at all. It was bright red. There were a dozen of them, glittering in a case in the center of the room. The Woburn Carbuncles— very pretty and doubtless worth a pretty penny.

"The Marquess of Tavistock discovered them in the attic, apparently," remarked Mr. Roberts.

Lucky marquess, I thought to myself. All we'd ever found in our attic was dry rot.

"Aren't they beautiful?" Mr. Roberts went on.

"This way!" Palis cried, and went on himself. We followed.

I was the last to leave the room. For some reason there were no tourists behind me. I thought it was strange. There had been at least twenty other people in every room we'd visited, but suddenly there was no one at all. I walked toward the door. At the same moment there was a crash of breaking glass. A bell went off. I turned and looked back.

It was impossible. A minute ago I'd been looking at a glass-topped cabinet with twelve red carbuncles inside. Now I was looking at a shattered cabinet with only eleven carbuncles lying in the wreckage. But apart from the security guards, there was nobody in the room. Someone had just stolen part of the Woburn windfall. The alarm bell was still ringing. But I knew it wasn't me and it couldn't have been them, so . . .

"All right, sonny. Stay where you are . . ."

The two guards were walking toward me, the splinters of glass crunching on the carpet beneath their feet. I looked over my shoulder. All the kids from the school were jammed into the doorway, staring at me.

"What's going on?" Palis called out from behind them.

"Give it back, son," the security guard muttered, holding out one hand. He was moving very slowly, like I was dangerous or something. "You can't get away with it."

"Get away with what?" I squeaked. My voice seemed to have climbed up my nose and hidden behind my eyes.

I pushed my hands into my pockets. I wanted to show them that they were empty, that it was all a terrible mistake. But before I could say another word, my palm came into contact with something cold and round. I took it out. It glittered in the sunlight.

"What . . . ?" Palis exclaimed.

"Wait a minute . . ." I said.

But it was clear that nobody had any intention of waiting a minute. If Palis didn't grab me, the guards would. The bell was still ringing and now I could hear other voices shouting in the corridor. Perhaps half a second passed—enough time for an instant playback and an even more instant decision. It was a frame-up. It had to be. Somebody had slipped the jewel into my pocket. Who? I remembered the guard jostling me as I went into the Grand Salon, the same guard who was now about six feet away from me and getting closer. It didn't make sense. But it had to be him. He'd been in the room. He'd seen . . .

An instant decision! I stuffed the jewel back in my pocket, turned, and ran.

The guard shouted something after me. Palis reached out. Somehow I twisted out of his grip and then I was pushing my way through my own friends, hoping that none of them would try to stop me. At least I was right about that. They did quite the opposite, crowding around the door and stopping Palis and the two guards who were already trying to force their way after me.

I paused for breath beside a window. At the same moment there was a sudden wailing and six police cars, blue lights flashing, tore up the drive and screeched to a halt outside. It was impossible. They couldn't possibly have gotten there that fast. My stomach shrank like a punctured football. It was a

frame-up all right. But it didn't just stop with the two security guards. It had been organized on a massive scale.

About a dozen policemen were scattering across the drive,
moving to surround the house. Palis had almost broken
through the barrier of schoolboys. This was no time to ask
questions. It was crazy, of course. Even if I could get out of
the house, I had nowhere to go. But right then I didn't care.
I just wanted to get out. I could ask questions later.

I looked round. I was in the State Dining Room. A dozen
dukes and duchesses stared down at me accusingly from the
walls. In the middle of the room there was a table set
for eight—eight guests who would never arrive. Perfect
white porcelain, gleaming silver cutlery, and slender glasses
stood on the polished surface to be admired by the passing
tourists. There was a door at the other end of the room. I
made for it.

But I hadn't taken two steps before my way was blocked.
One of the antique ladies, roused by the bell and the shouting, stood there, holding a half-finished pink cardigan on two
knitting needles. She was about sixty, dressed in a two-piece
suit with permed hair and two angry red spots in her cheeks.

"Stop him!" Palis yelled out behind me.

The old lady's lips pouted in anger. She must have
thought I was a vandal or something. "Oh, you beast!" she
exclaimed. "You little beast!"

She jerked her hands. The pink cardigan fell to the ground

and suddenly she was holding the two knitting needles above her head as if they were daggers, the points pointing at me.

"You beast!" she shrilled for a third time, and, with her eyes blazing, charged toward me. At the same time I ran toward her.

About one second later we met.

I didn't mean to do it. I don't know what I meant to do. But she could have killed me with those needles and I had to defend myself. As she stabbed downward, I ducked. My shoulder went into her stomach in a sort of crazy football tackle. I heaved upward. And then she was soaring through the air, carried by her own momentum, a whirling mass of tweed suit, nylon stocking, and stainless-steel knitting needles. With a little screech she landed on the dinner table, then slid all the way down with an explosion of shattering plates and glasses and clattering knives and forks. The polished wood offered no resistance. She shot off the other end like a rocket, hit the wall, and finally disappeared as, with a resounding crash, one of the portraits fell on top of her. I didn't see what state she was in after that. I was already gone.

I found myself in yet another, smaller room—some sort of library. A third guard was struggling out of his chair as I approached. I pushed him back with the flat of my hand and sighed as he crashed into a shelf, instantly disappearing in an avalanche of books. There was a long corridor leading off with a window at the end. I opened it and climbed out.

The window led onto a narrow balcony running along the side of the house. My luck was still holding out. There was nobody in sight. Quickly, I hoisted myself over the edge, clinging on with both hands. For a moment I hung there. Then I dropped. It was a long way. A bank of grass broke my fall. It also broke my leg—at least, that's what it felt like. When I got up I found I could barely stand. I'd twisted my ankle and torn my trousers. But at least I was out.

I limped round to the back of the house and through a wrought-iron gate. I had got as far as the parking lot before I realized that I had no idea where I was going. After all, I couldn't just get onto the bus and expect them to take me back to school. And running was out of the question.

Quite apart from my ankle, the fields around Woburn Abbey were flat and wide. I'd be spotted a mile away. Worse still, the police were streaming out of the building, spreading out and searching for me.

And everything I'd done up to now had only made matters worse. Perhaps I could have explained away the jewel in my pocket. Even if they hadn't believed me, I could have put it down to a schoolboy prank. I could have told them I was going to give it to charity. But I'd also hurled an old lady through the air. I'd smashed hundreds of dollars' worth of plates and glass. How could this have happened to me?

Desperately I looked around; at the cars parked in neat rows, at the families strolling toward the abbey wondering what all the fuss was about, at the first policemen rapidly approaching. I was thinking on my feet. I could barely stand on my feet. My ankle was doing a good impersonation of a beach ball. I had nowhere to go, no way of getting there.

Then I saw the Land Rover. It was parked at the end of a row, with no one around. The doors would be locked, of course, but there was something on the roof, covered with a sheet of tarpaulin. But the tarpaulin hadn't been tied down properly. There was a gap.

Without a second thought I climbed up the back of the Land Rover and crawled through. There were a whole lot of sacks on the roof, filled with some sort of grain. Either the driver was a farmer or a health-food fanatic. There was just enough space for me. I lay there in the darkness, listening to my heart thumping. I'd just made it in time. I heard the crunch of footsteps on gravel.

"You see him?" somebody asked.

"No."

"Thirteen years old. Scruffy. And dangerous."

"Try over there . . ."

About two minutes later there were more footsteps and the sound of a man and a woman talking in low voices. I heard the Land Rover doors open and close. There was a rattle as the engine started and the whole vehicle shook. Then I felt myself pressed against the sacks as the Land Rover jerked forward. We were away!

Given more time, the police might have set up a roadblock and searched every car as it left the abbey. But we weren't stopped as we trundled out, traveling at about ten miles an hour. I couldn't see anything under the tarpaulin and I didn't dare look. I just hoped that wherever the Land Rover was heading it was somewhere a long way away—preferably New Zealand. I imagined we'd hit the M1 pretty soon. After that I'd be safe, at least for the time being.

But we didn't go anywhere near the highway. The driver seemed to be in no hurry. Ten minutes later we were still moving along at a snail's pace. It was getting hot under the tarpaulin with the sun beating down. I could hardly breathe. Carefully I reached out, lifted up the loose flap, and looked out.

We were in a traffic jam—just what I needed. There were at least six cars behind us. I couldn't see how many more in front. The road was following a tall silver fence with a second, lower fence behind it. Otherwise all I could see were fields and trees.

Stop and start, stop and start. We didn't seem to be going anywhere and we were taking an awful long time getting there. I peeked out again, just in time to read a notice on a wooden board beside the road. PLEASE PUT YOUR RADIO ANTENNAS DOWN, it said. Put your antennas down? Where was the road leading? Under a low bridge?

The Land Rover stopped again. I didn't dare look out, but I heard voices.

"Have you got any pets in the car?" a woman asked.

"No." That was the driver.

"Here you are . . ."

"Thank you."

So we weren't carrying any pets. That was really nice to know. But what had that got to do with anything? Where were we? I was almost suffocating. We were still crawling along and the sun was hotter than ever. By now I'd decided to clear off at the first opportunity. Getting onto the Land Rover had been a mistake in the first place. I'd just have to leg it cross-country.

About another fifteen minutes passed before I'd had enough. We'd stopped and started more times than I could count and I had no idea where I was. But at least I was out of the abbey. Throwing caution to the wind, I shifted on the roof and slithered out from under the tarpaulin. Without looking around, I dropped to the grass. My ankle screamed at me. Ignoring it, I ran.

Only when I was sixty feet from the Land Rover did I stop and take my bearings.

I was in a field, penned in. A fence ran the whole length, boarded at the top, like something in a prison. The Land Rover was standing in line with about a dozen cars on either side. A picnic area. That was my first thought. But why should anyone want to have a picnic here? It was a rough, uneven field with knotted grass and bumpy hillocks. A few trees twisted upward here and there. The road we'd been following zig-zagged all the way from the fence. I looked at the cars. Despite the weather, all the windows were rolled up. The people inside were waving at me and pointing. They didn't look like they were inviting me to a picnic.

Then a loudspeaker crackled into life and a voice echoed across the grass.

"Get back into the car!" it commanded. "Get back into the car!"

And at the same time I heard a low, angry growling that sent my heart scuttling into my mouth and made the hairs on the back of my neck stand up like a pincushion. I turned around. A full-size lion was padding slowly toward me.

I still don't know how I managed to avoid wetting myself. I couldn't believe what I'd just done. I'd sat on top of a Land Rover and let it drive me straight into the middle of the safari park. Where else do you go after you've visited Woburn Abbey? And then, when we were nicely settled in the lion compound, I'd gotten off. Couldn't I at least have waited for the giraffes? Giraffes are vegetarians. The lion obviously wasn't.

It was snarling at me, its mouth open. I could see all the way down the back of its throat. Any minute now I'd be getting an inside view. The lion was huge. You could have made twenty furry hot-water bottles out of its mane alone. But that wasn't what I was looking at. I was looking at its teeth: horrible, sharp teeth glistening in the sunlight. And the lion was looking at me. Its ugly brown eyes were burning with anger. And hunger.

It can't be much fun being a lion in a safari park. All day long you sit there watching your lunch drive past in little metal boxes. Canned food. Well, this food had just gotten out of the can.

There was an orange-and-black Jeep tearing across the grass toward me. But by the time it arrived it would be too late. I wanted to run for it, but there was no chance. The other cars were too far away and my legs had turned to jelly . . . jelly that hadn't even set. The lion growled again, about to leap. I was alone, unarmed.

Unarmed . . .

Suddenly I remembered the slingshot that I'd found on the coach. My hand fumbled its way into my pocket and pulled it out. All I needed was a stone, some sort of missile. But there were no stones. Just grass and a few twigs. The lion edged forward. There was nothing in sight. Not even a pebble.

And then I remembered the Woburn Carbuncle.

I'd pulled it out before I even realized what I was doing. It glittered, a brilliant red, about the size of a Ping-Pong ball. The lion's snarl became a roar. My hand was shaking like a leaf but somehow I managed to load the slingshot, pulled on the rubber band. The lion leaped. I fired.

It was still roaring, its mouth open, as the carbuncle flashed through the air. At the same time I threw myself to one side.

The carbuncle disappeared down the lion's throat.

I rolled over and looked around. The lion had missed me by about half a yard. It was lying on its back and for a crazy moment I was reminded of Sington in the bus with the chewing gum. The carbuncle had lodged itself in the creature's windpipe. It was kicking its legs feebly in the air, choking and whimpering like a stray cat. Weakly, I got to my feet.

I just had time to see another three lions come strolling over the hill to find out what was happening when the Jeep arrived. A warden was standing up in the passenger seat, aiming a rifle with an anesthetic dart. He fired and missed. There was a sharp pain in my thigh and the world began to spin.

I blacked out. But before I went, I realized that the warden hadn't missed after all. He'd been aiming at me all the time! He must have decided that I was more dangerous than the lion.

TRIAL AND ERROR

In the end I was accused of theft, assault, trespassing, criminal damage, and cruelty to animals. The lion survived, by the way. It was on the operating table for six hours to remove the carbuncle. The bad news for the surgeon was that it woke up after five.

I was sent to the Old Bailey to be tried—number three court. I still remember it. It was far smaller than I'd imagined it would be, walled in with wooden panels but with clear glass windows in the roof. It was like standing in a cross between a chapel and a squash court. The jury sat along one side—twelve men just and true. They may have been true but half the time they were only just awake. And in the middle there was a whole cluster of barristers and court officials in their black robes and white bows, looking like the sort of gift-wrapped packages you might take to a funeral.

I was in the dock, of course, with two burly policemen close behind me. Counsel for the prosecution couldn't even glance at me without grinding his teeth. The judge was too old to have any teeth but looked like he'd have been glad to grind someone else's. As for my counsel for the defense, he kept on sighing and mopping his face with a handkerchief. He knew a hopeless case when he saw one.

To be honest, I found the whole thing a bit of a trial. Which is to say it was about as interesting as a double period of algebra on a wet afternoon. These legal people seemed to take an hour to say what you and I could manage in a minute. They couldn't even say good morning without written evidence from the weather office.

Things livened up, though, when the witnesses arrived. First on was the old lady from Woburn Abbey—now in tweed neck brace and matching splints. She described how I'd attacked her and thrown her along the dinner table only somehow she forgot to mention that she'd been the one with the knitting needles.

"What happened after you hit the table?" counsel for the defense asked.

"An old master fell on me."

"Are you referring to the Marquess of Tavistock?"

"No," she sniffed. "It was a painting."

That brought a titter of laughter from the public gallery. The judge banged his gavel and not for the first time I was tempted to shout out, *Sold to the lady with the neck brace and knitting needles.* But I kept my mouth shut.

"No further questions," defense muttered miserably.

The prosecution called two more security guards and the ranger from the safari park. They all told much the same story. I'd been caught red-handed with the carbuncle. I'd fought my way out. I'd half killed a lion. I'd finally been arrested. I was just grateful they didn't call the lion.

Then it was the turn of the defense.

My counsel was a thin, gray-haired man called Wilson. We'd met before the trial and I'd asked him how he was going to get me off the hook. He'd laughed at that. He didn't laugh often. You almost expected to see cobwebs at the corners of his mouth.

"Get you off?" he asked. "I can't get you off. The evidence against you is overwhelming. It's rock solid. It's massive!"

"But I was framed."

"So was the old lady you attacked. A picture fell on her." He mopped himself with the handkerchief. "All I can do is persuade the judge that, at heart, you're a nice boy," he said. He looked at me and wrinkled his nose. "Of course, that won't be easy. But this is a first offense. Perhaps he'll go easy on you."

"How easy?" I asked.

Wilson shrugged. "Six months . . . ?"

"Prison!" I stared at him. "I can't go to prison! I'm innocent!"

"Of course." He sighed. "Until you're proven guilty."

So Wilson set out to prove that, despite appearances, I was a nice boy. Unfortunately for me, he'd chosen the wrong witnesses. I knew this the moment I saw the first of them. It was my brother Tim.

He'd dressed up in a suit for the occasion and I noticed he was wearing a black tie. Had he put it on by accident, or did he know something I didn't? I could see that he was trembling like a leaf. Anyone would think *he* was on trial.

The court bailiff handed him a Bible. Tim took it, nodded, and tried to put it in his pocket. The bailiff snatched it back. I thought there was going to be another fight, but then the judge explained that Tim was meant to use the Bible to take the oath. Tim blushed.

"Sorry, Your Highness," he muttered.

The judge frowned. "You can address me as 'Your Worship.'"

"Oh yes . . ." Tim was going to pieces and he hadn't exactly been together to start with. "Sorry, Your Highship."

The bailiff moved forward and tried again.

"I swear to tell the truth," he said.

"Do you?" Tim asked.

"No—you do!" The bailiff closed his eyes.

"Just repeat the words, Mr. Diamond." The judge sighed.

At last the oath was taken. Wilson got up and walked over to the witness box, moving like an old man. Tim smiled at him.

"You are Herbert Timothy Diamond?" Wilson asked.

"Am I?" Tim sounded astonished.

"Are you Herbert Timothy Diamond?" the judge demanded.

"Yes . . . yes, of course I am, Your Parsnip," Tim said.

Wilson took a deep breath. "Could you describe your brother for us?" he asked.

"Well, he's about five-foot-two, dark hair, quite thin . . ."

Counsel for the defense shuddered and I thought he was going to have some sort of attack. His cheeks were pinched and his wig was crooked. "We know what he looks like, Mr. Diamond," he whimpered. "We just want to know what sort of person he is."

Tim thought for a minute.

"Answer the question," the judge muttered.

"Certainly, Your Cowslip," Tim said. "Nick's all right. I mean . . . for a kid brother. The one trouble is, he's really untidy. He's always leaving his books in the kitchen and—"

"We are not interested in your kitchen!" Wilson groaned. He was fighting to keep his patience. But it was a losing battle. "What we want to know is, looking at him now, would you say he had it in him to brutally assault an old lady and steal a priceless jewel?"

Tim gave me a big smile and nodded. "Oh yes. Absolutely!"

Wilson was about to ask another question but now he stopped, his mouth wide open. "You can't say that!" he squeaked. "He's your brother!"

"But you told me to tell the truth," Tim protested. "The truth, the whole truth, and nothing but the truth."

There was another uproar in the court. The judge banged his gavel. Tim had cooked my goose all right—feathers and all. After his testimony, the judge would throw the book at me. But that was nothing compared with what I planned to throw at Tim.

Wilson sank back into his seat. "No more questions," he said.

"Does that mean I can leave the witless box?" Tim asked. Nobody stopped him. The trial was more or less over.

The jury took forty-five seconds to reach its verdict. Guilty, of course. Then it was time for the sentence. The policemen made me stand up. The judge glared at me.

"Nicholas Martin Simple," he began. "You have been found guilty on all five charges. It is now my duty to sentence you.

"Your crime was a particularly unpleasant one. You are, if I may say, a particularly unpleasant criminal. You stole a priceless object, part of the national heritage. You viciously assaulted an old lady and a lion. You caused thousands of dollars' worth of damage. And for what? Doubtless you would have squandered your profits on pop music, on violent video-cassettes, on glue, which you would then sniff."

He sniffed himself. Then he bent his fingers until the bones clicked.

"Society must be protected from the likes of you," he went on. "If you were older, the sentence would be more severe. As it is, it is the sentence of this court that you will go to a young offenders' institution, for eighteen months." He banged his hammer. "Court adjourned."

Things happened very quickly after that.

The two policemen dragged me out of the courtroom, down a flight of stairs. My hands were cuffed in front of me and I was led along a passage to a door. Outside, in an un-derground parking garage, a van was waiting.

"In you go," one of the policemen said.

On my way up—before I'd been tried—I'd been "son" or "Nick." Now I didn't have a name. A hand pushed me in the small of my back. And my back had never felt smaller. It was like I'd somehow shrunk.

"But I'm innocent," I mumbled.

The policemen ignored me.

Two of them got in after me. The doors were locked and the van drove away. There was one small window in the back, heavily barred. The frosted glass broke the whole world up into teardrops. We reached the surface. The Old Bailey, Holborn . . . London slipped away behind me. The policemen didn't speak. One of them was reading a newspaper. My own face smiled at me from the front page.

But I wasn't smiling now. It had begun to rain. The wa-ter was pattering down on the tin roof like somebody had dropped a bag of marbles. The policeman yawned and turned a page. I shifted in my seat and the handcuffs clinked.

We drove for almost an hour, heading west. Then we slowed down. I saw a gate slide shut behind us. The van stopped. We had arrived.

The prison was an ugly Victorian building: rust-colored bricks and a gray slate roof. It was shaped like a square with a wall running all the way around and a watchtower at each corner. The watchtowers were connected to the main building by metal drawbridges, which could be raised or lowered automatically. A glass-fronted guardhouse stood beside the central control gate.

I was led in through a door in the side of the prison. And suddenly it was as if I'd stepped off the planet. All the street sounds, even the whisper of the wind, had been cut out. The air smelled of sweat and machine oil. The door clicked shut.

The policemen led me to a counter where a man in guard's uniform was waiting for me.

"Simple?" the guard asked.

"That's him," the policeman said.

"All right."

The two policemen left.

I was told to empty my pockets. Everything I owned—even my watch—was taken from me and put in a cardboard box marked with my name. The guard wrote it all down on a sheet of paper.

"Two dollars in loose change. One pen. One lucky rabbit's foot"—he smiled mirthlessly—"obviously not working. One bag of salt and vinegar chips, half eaten. A rubber band . . ." He made me sign for them, then told me to strip. My clothes went into the box and he handed me a pile of blue denim and white cotton with a pair of boots balanced on the top.

"Now you take a shower," he said.

"But I've already had a shower."

"Just do as you're told."

I took a shower. A medical examination followed. I was poked, prodded, and injected. My hair was cut. Finally, I was allowed to dress. The shirt was too small and the boots were too big, but somehow I didn't think the prison authorities were interested in the latest fashion. After that, a second guard appeared. There was a chain looping down the side of his trousers all the way to his knee.

"This way, 95446," he said.

95446—that was the number stenciled on the front of my new jacket. That was me.

I was taken down a corridor lined with doors—all locked. The last door was mine. The guard took out a key and opened it.

"In," he said. He wasn't the talkative sort.

The cell was about six by twelve feet—bare bricks, a tiny window, two chairs, a table, a washbasin, a bucket, and a pair of bunk beds. A figure rolled off the lower bunk and gave me a crooked smile.

"Welcome to Strangeday Hall, kid," he said. "I'm Johnny Powers."

JOHNNY POWERS

"Welcome to Strangeday Hall. I'm Johnny Powers."

The words hadn't been spoken in a friendly way. The voice was cold, mocking—with a twist of Irish in the accent. My cell mate perched on the edge of the bunk, chewing a stick of licorice. I looked at him and my mouth went dry. I'd seen some nasties in my time, but this guy was something else again.

He was about the same height as me although he was two years older, thickset and fleshy. He had small, ugly eyes, a small, upturned nose, and a narrow mouth set in a permanent sneer. He wore his hair greased back, the hairline snaking across his brow. His skin was pale and lifeless. Maybe he'd spent too much time out of the sun. Or maybe he was already dead but people had been too afraid to mention it to him.

That was the most frightening thing about him—his age-lessness. I knew he was fifteen, but he had the face of a baby. Chubby cheeks and perfect teeth. His eyelashes could have been painted on with a brush. Yet when he smiled (he was smiling at me now) there was suddenly an old man sitting there, an old man who liked killing people. I wondered how many people had left this world with that smile fading in their eyes.

This was Johnny Powers. Public Enemy Number One. He had hitchhiked his way out of somebody's nightmare.

"Hi," I said. "I'm Nick Diamond."

"Diamond—huh?" He took a bite out of the licorice. "What are you in for?"

"A jewel robbery," I said. I was in no mood to explain. "The Woburn Carbuncles."

"Is that so?" His eyes twinkled and he looked genuinely pleased. "Now ya mention it, I remember reading something about it." The face hardened. "But just don't get any bright ideas while you're here, kid. I'm number one in this joint. Ya do things my way. Or ya never do nothing again."

"Sure. Absolutely."

Well, what else could I say to him? Johnny Powers was obviously so far around the bend that he was coming back around the other side.

I threw my few possessions onto the top bunk.

"What happened to your last cell mate?" I asked.

Powers smiled his crooked smile. "He and I didn't get along so good," he said. "So one night he jumped out of the window."

I glanced at the window. "But it's barred," I said.

"Yeah. He jumped out one piece at a time." Powers screwed the licorice into his mouth. "Maybe I gave him a little help. Know what I mean?" He giggled. "Ya need any help, just ask."

"I'll let you know," I said.

A bell rang then and the cell door opened. I looked at my watch, remembered it wasn't there, and followed Powers out. There were kids streaming out of the cells on both sides of the corridor and above me, too. They were all in identical uniforms, the same uniform that I was wearing. None of them were over sixteen. None of them were smiling. There must have been three hundred of them. Three hundred of *us.* I kept on having to remind myself that I was one of them . . . would be for the next year and a half.

We marched through a door and into a large hall with long tables set in two rows and a balcony at one end where an armed guard stood watching us. A notice hung on one wall: PRISONERS ARE FORBIDDEN TO TALK DURING MEALTIME.

A few minutes later I got my first taste of prison food. Taste is the wrong word. It didn't have any. We lined up at a hatch where we were served watery stew, mashed potatoes and cabbage, prunes and custard. Shut your eyes and you wouldn't know which was which. I didn't like to think what animal had ended its days in the stew. All I can say is that it had a lot of fat, not a lot of meat, and some sort of disease.

Nobody talked and for ten minutes the only sound was the clatter of spoons and forks against tin trays. I didn't eat anything. I'd left my appetite in the number three court of the Old Bailey. It was probably still sitting in the dock, dreaming of a Big Mac. Another bell rang and we carried the trays back to the hatch.

I'd just handed mine over when there was a crackle from

a loudspeaker and a voice called out. "Nine-five-four-four-six Simple to the visitor's room."

Powers was right behind me. "Well, whaddya know," he whispered. "Only been here five minutes and ya got callers."

A guard appeared and led me back through the door, down a corridor, up a flight of stairs, and into another room.

"So you finally ended up where you belong," Chief Inspector Snape said.

Of course I'd expected to see him sooner or later. Snape had set it all up from the start. He'd asked me to share a cell with Johnny Powers, and when I'd refused he'd gone ahead and arranged it anyway. He must have found out about the trip to Woburn Abbey. Somehow he'd held the other tourists back so that I'd be alone in the room with the carbuncles. One of his men had already slipped the jewel into my jacket pocket. Another had smashed the cabinet. After that I more or less played into his hands—or at least, his handcuffs.

And here he was, sitting at a table, smoking. Boyle stood behind him, grinning at me like he'd just heard some great joke. Only I was the joke. Well, they hadn't heard anything yet. Did they really expect me to take all this sitting down?

"Sit down," Snape said.

"Snape—" I began.

"Take a seat, laddie," he interrupted. "I can understand you're a bit cut up, but—"

"Cut up?" I almost screamed at him. "What do you mean 'cut up'? I've been sent to a detention center. I've got eighteen months. Eighteen months! I'll be lucky if I manage eighteen minutes! I'm sharing a cell with a loony. And you know what happened to his last cell mate? Yeah—he was 'cut up' all right. Into lots of pieces!"

He waited until I'd finished, then gestured at the chair. Boyle nodded, the smile still on his face. Wearily I sat down.

"I need a job done," Snape said.

"A job," Boyle muttered.

"Powers could be the only chance I have of getting to the Fence. I told you I have to find him."

"And I told you—no!" I sighed. "You could have found someone else to do it for you."

Snape shook his head. "There was nobody else. It had to be you, laddie. You're thirteen, and you're smart. And the trouble is, we don't have much time."

"Time?" I almost laughed. "Well, I've got plenty of time. Eighteen months . . ."

Snape shook his head again. "I'm afraid not. You see I've just got the latest psychiatric reports on Powers."

"And what do the psychiatrists say?"

"They don't say anything. They're too frightened to be in the same room as him. They won't go anywhere near him. He's violent. Homicidal—"

"I noticed."

"—and he's getting worse. Any day he could crack up altogether. After that he'll be useless to me. A vegetable . . ."

"I don't get the problem," I said. "It's never stopped you working with Boyle."

At least that finally wiped the smile off Boyle's face. He lumbered toward me, his hands outstretched.

"No, Boyle," Snape sighed.

"I'll kill him . . ."

"No!"

"I'll say it was an accident," Boyle pleaded. "I'll say he was resisting arrest."

"How can he be resisting arrest when he's already in prison?" Snape demanded.

Boyle had no answer to that. He went off to sulk in the corner.

"What was that you were saying about violent and homicidal?" I asked.

Snape glanced at his deputy then turned back to me. "You have to get the name out of Powers while he can still talk," he said. "One name. That's all we want."

"And what if I refuse?"

He shrugged. "Then you're here for another seventeen months and thirty days."

"Wait a minute . . . !"

"No. You wait a minute, laddie." Snape leaned across the table. "Only two people in the world know that you didn't really steal the Woburn Carbuncle. Boyle and me."

"What about the security guards?"

"You'll never find them. We got you in here. Only we can get you out. But if you refuse to cooperate . . ." He left the sentence hanging in the air. Right then I'd have liked to have seen him hanging in the air beside it.

I stood up.

"The Fence," I said.

"Get close to Powers . . ."

"Close?" I cried. "If I got any closer we'd be sharing the same bed." I took a deep breath. Snape had beaten me and he knew it. "All right," I said. "You win. I'll find out what you want to know. But if you don't get me out of here . . ."

"Relax." Suddenly Snape was all smiles again. He dug a hand into his pocket and pulled something out. He threw it down on the table. "Have a bar of chocolate on us, laddie," he said. "Boyle bought it for you. Thick and nutty."

"Yeah." I gazed at the two of them and sighed. "I couldn't have put it better myself."

Powers was waiting for me when I got back to the cell. He was rolling a cigarette. A chocolate one.

"So who was it?" he asked.

"The police," I said. I'd been practicing my answer on the way. "They just wanted to ask me more questions."

It was the first time I'd lied to Johnny Powers and he almost seemed to sense it like a dog scenting blood. He looked at me curiously, the skin under his eyes tightening. But he didn't say anything. Not yet. Sometime later the lights went out. There were no good-nights. Nobody came to tuck me in. The darkness just cut in without argument. And that was all.

My first night in Strangeday Hall. I undressed and climbed onto the top bunk, pulling the rough blankets and even rougher sheet over me. The pillow was as soft as cardboard. There was a full moon that night, spilling in through the window. A perfect square of light perched on the wall, cut into sections by the black shadows of the bars. In the distance, a plane screamed through the sky.

I lay there for an hour. I couldn't sleep. There was only one way out of this mess, and the sooner it started, the better. Cursing Snape, I opened my eyes.

"Powers?" I said.

"Yeah?" He sounded wide-awake, too.

"I just want you to know . . . I really admire you. I read about you in all the papers. I always hoped I could join up with you."

"Is that so?" I couldn't tell if he believed me. His voice was cold, empty.

I swallowed and went on. "When I stole that jewel . . . I had a slingshot in my pocket. Like your gang—the Slingshot Kids."

"We never had no slingshots."

"Sure, Powers. But I couldn't afford a shotgun. That's why I was stealing the jewel." There was no answer. "I'd have gotten away if you'd been there. And then we could have sold the jewel. It was worth thousands. The only thing is, I didn't know who to sell it to. What would you have done, Powers?"

There was a long silence. I didn't even hear him get out of bed. But a second later he was standing up with his head close to mine, the moon dancing in his eyes.

"Listen, Diamond," he said. "I don't know ya and what I don't know I don't trust. Maybe you're on the level. If not, ya'll end buried underneath it. Know what I mean?"

He stared at me. There was still something of the choirboy in his face. But it was a choirboy who would burn down the church sooner than sing in it.

"Ya want some advice?" he said. "Act like a shirt."

"Like a shirt?"

"Yeah. Button it."

Then he was gone. I turned over and shut my eyes. But the sun was already rising before I got any sleep.

INSIDE

Three weeks after I'd arrived at Strangeday Hall, Tim sent me a cake. He'd made it himself with eggs, flour, sugar, a hint of ginger, and a Black & Decker electric drill. The drill was buried in the middle. I guess it was his idea of the Great Escape. He needn't have bothered. Hiding a drill in a cake wasn't such a bad thought, but he could have put it in there after he'd baked it. By the time it came out of the oven there was as much cake in the drill as there was drill in the cake. And he forgot to enclose a bit.

Mind you, it was about the only good joke in the first month. There I was, surrounded by some of the toughest thugs and heavies in the country—people who would break your arms as soon as look at you. And that was just the guards. Most of the inmates were okay, although I did have an unfortunate run-in with a pickpocket. I didn't have any money, of course. But he stole my pockets.

What can I say about life on the inside? Perhaps you've heard that phrase "a short, sharp shock." Well, Strangeday Hall was more of a long-drawn-out surprise. It was the only juvenile prison in England like it. And I can tell you now, I didn't like it at all.

Up at six in the morning. Lukewarm showers—or stone-cold if Luke had forgotten to turn them on. Breakfast: a mug of tea, two slices of bread, and one slice of porridge. Then work until lunchtime—in the library, in the laundry, or in the classroom.

Lunch was at twelve. Stomachaches were at half past. After that we were allowed two hours' exercise. Sports were encouraged at Strangeday Hall. But not all sports. Cross-country running, for example, had been crossed off the agenda after the junior team made it to Scandinavia during the interprison finals.

We were locked in our cells until dinner . . . and that was where I'd come in. Dinner finished at six-thirty and then we were locked up again until the lights went out at ten. One day—any day—in the life of a jailbird. Because all of them were always the same.

But I was still working on Johnny Powers, my express ticket out. You'd have thought I'd have been able to get somewhere with him after four weeks in the same cell. But you'd be wrong. He was about as suspicious as a snake in a handbag factory and twice as poisonous. I was playing the tough kid, anxious to learn from him. All I wanted was one name— the Fence. All I got was monosyllables and sneers.

Worse still, he was cracking up fast. He got these headaches. One minute he'd be sitting there vandalizing a good book. The next he'd be curled up with his head in his hands, groaning and sweating. I tried offering him aspirin but he didn't even hear me. That was when I found out about his mother. He might have sold his granny to the salt mines, but he still loved his mother. He'd call out for her. And hours later, when the headache had gone but she hadn't come, he would sit there, hunched up, sucking his thumb. I could see what Snape meant. Powers needed a new jacket. The sort with the sleeves that button up behind the back. Another few weeks and he'd be swapping his cell for one with padded walls. And where would that leave me?

Everything changed one afternoon. I was on cleaning duty. I'd cleaned the kitchen, the dining hall, and two corridors and they were still pretty filthy. At Strangeday Hall you could never get rid of the dirt. You could just rearrange it. It was late in the afternoon and I thought I'd finished, but then one of the screws came up to me. His name was Walsh.

We called him "Weasel" on account of his thin face, his pointed nose, and his little mustache. He didn't like me. He didn't much like anyone.

"Finished, 95446?" he asked.

"Yes, sir, Mr. Walsh." I smiled at him. "Why don't you call me 954 for short?" I said. "It's more friendly."

He stared at me, his left eye twitching. "Are you trying to be funny, 95446?" he asked.

"No, Mr. Walsh."

"Now the showers. I want them spotless."

"But, Mr. Walsh—"

"Are you arguing, 95446?"

"No, Mr. Walsh."

Prison officers and teachers have a lot in common.

It must have been about half past four when I set out across the yard to the showers, which were in a low building on the other side. All the other inmates were either in the class-rooms or locked up in their cells. High above me, the guards looked down from their metal watchtowers, fingering their automatic rifles like I was a duck in a fairground. Scratch one Diamond and win a goldfish. I looked up at them and waved. Somebody telephoned the central-control guardhouse and a moment later the door to the shower cubicles clicked open.

The door led into a white-tiled room with hooks and benches where we undressed. From here a long corridor stretched down to the far wall with metal cubicles on both sides. The showers were regulated by three huge taps in a maze of pipes, valves, and gauges close to the changing room. The whole system must have been out-of-date the day it was built. And that day must have been sometime before the Victorians.

I'd thought I'd be alone there, but I hadn't taken two steps before I heard voices, low and threatening, behind the drip of the water. Carefully, I put down my bucket and mop, then edged toward the corridor. There was something about the voices that I didn't like, and I couldn't even hear what they were saying yet. But nobody was meant to be in the showers. If they'd sneaked in in the middle of the afternoon, it wasn't because they fancied a wash.

I reached the corridor and slipped behind the first of the

partitions, next to the taps. From here I could get a better view. With my cheek pressed against the cold metal, I peered around. What I saw was even worse than I had expected. And at Strangeday Hall expectations were always pretty bad.

Johnny Powers was there, slumped against the far wall. It was difficult to see in the half-light, but I could tell he'd taken a beating. He was sitting like a broken doll. Nobody had scratched their initials into him yet, but his nose was bleeding and for once his hair was ruffled. There were three guys with him.

I recognized them at once, even with their backs to me, and my mouth went dry.

The tallest of them was Mark White—three years for armed robbery. He was the most crooked con in the joint: crooked shoulders, crooked hips, and a crooked smile. With him was a Scottish guy, McNeil. He was small with greasy hair and a pronounced stomach . . . which he pronounced "stumma." Half the time you couldn't understand what he was saying. Most of the time you didn't want to. I didn't know what the third guy was in for. His name was Blondie, and it was true he had blond hair. But you could have also called him Ugly and you'd have been right there, too. Somebody once told me he'd murdered his dentist. If I'd had teeth like his, I'd have probably murdered mine.

"Aren't you going to call for help, Johnny?" White was saying. I could hear them all now. "Maybe one of the screws will hear you."

"I don't need help from no one." Powers spat blood.

"Let him have it," Blondie hissed. "Do it now."

"Yeah—do it now." Powers giggled. "Whassa matter, White? Mebbe ya're a bit yellow, too. White and yellow—like an egg."

White moved to one side. That was when I saw what he was carrying. I couldn't believe it. Just about every prisoner at Strangeday Hall had a weapon of some sort, usually home-made daggers or "shanks," as they were called. But White had gone one better. Somehow he'd gotten hold of a gun. And he was pointing it at Powers.

"You're going to get it, Johnny," he said. "But not yet." He glanced upward. "I reckon you've got another couple of minutes . . ."

Another couple of minutes. My mind was racing. What would happen in another couple of minutes? Then I realized. The prison was on the flight path to Heathrow. They were waiting for a plane to drown out the sound of the gunshot. It was the perfect cover. Johnny Powers would be drowned and shot at the same time.

If it had been anybody else, I might have just backed out then and there. It was none of my business who was shooting who or why. But this was Powers. I had no choice. I had to get him out of there—and in one piece.

I looked around me. I don't know what I expected to find. An automatic rifle accidentally left there by one of the guards?

If so, I was out of luck. All I could see was a broken shoelace and an old towel lying in a puddle of water.

"Two minutes, Johnny," White said. "You got any last-minute requests?"

"Yeah. Drop dead."

That was typical Powers. If he'd made a request on the radio it would have been for "The Funeral March."

But looking at the towel had given me an idea. Moving as quietly as I could, I went over and examined the Victorian plumbing system. There were three taps—one for hot water, one for cold. The third controlled the pressure. There was also a gauge with pipes snaking in and out, a circular clock-face with a big slice of red. I guessed the system had never been turned to full pressure. The whole thing would proba-bly explode.

Well, there was always a first time . . .

I gripped the tap. The metal was cool and damp against the palm of my hand. Hoping it wouldn't squeak, I gave it a quarter turn to the right. There was a loud shudder. The pipes coughed and water gurgled like a man with indigestion.

"Whassat?" McNeil asked. He'd heard it, too. He'd have had to be deaf to miss it.

"It's nothing," White replied, and I breathed again. "Just the pipes."

I turned the tap again. It made two complete revolutions before it tightened, fully open. All the pipes were bubbling and groaning now. I looked at the pressure gauge. The needle had jerked up like a conductor's baton. Already it was vertical, and even as I watched, it began to shiver toward the right.

"You sure?" McNeil asked again. He had a sulking, unhappy voice.

"Go check it out if you're so worried," White replied.

"I wanna ask ya something," Powers said suddenly.

"What is it?" White said.

"Who put ya up to this?" Powers demanded. "Who sent ya the gun? I'd just like to know."

"Who do you think?" White asked. There was a pause. "Big Ed."

"Big Ed?"

"Yeah. He figured it's time you kinda left the scene. Permanently. Know what I mean?"

"Well, whaddya know?" Powers muttered. "Big Ed . . ."

But then he stopped. I could hear another sound now, even louder than the pipes. It was a distant whine getting louder and closer by the second.

A plane was coming in to land. And time had just run out for Johnny Powers.

"Here it comes," White said. "Say your prayers, Johnny."

I reached for the towel, picked it up, slapped it against the hot tap. Even with the wet material, I could feel the metal burning underneath. The showers might have been lukewarm for us, but right now they were white-hot.

I glanced at the pressure gauge. The needle had passed right through the red section and was trying to find a way out on the other side. The whine of the plane had become a roar. Clutching the tap through the towel, I turned it as fast as I could.

Then everything happened at once.

There was a great hiss as the water rushed through the taps. All the showers sprang into life at once, boiling water spraying out in all directions. The pipes rattled and shook like they were trying to tear themselves out of the wall. Steam filled the room, a sudden impenetrable fog.

"What the . . . ?" White began.

Then one of the showers exploded, the head shooting across the room like a bullet. Steam and water bellowed out in a jet.

The plane was right overhead now. The whole building was vibrating. There was a gunshot. Even at that close range I hardly heard it. Then a second shower blew itself apart, unable to bear the pressure. Blondie screamed, his face disappearing in a blast of white heat.

I'd wrapped the towel around my face and I was on my knees, crawling underneath the swirling clouds. I couldn't see anything. I could hardly hear anything. The pipes were slamming against the wall in a frenzy. Three more showers exploded. Burning water cascaded onto my back.

"Johnny!" I called out. My voice was muffled by the towel.

Then there was a splat of fist against flesh and a figure flew through the mist, crashed into a cubicle, and slumped beside me. It was White. He was out cold—about the only thing in the building that was cold. He no longer had the gun.

Then somebody else lurched out of the steam on all fours. This time it was Powers. Miraculously, he didn't seem to have been burned.

"Good work, kid," he said. There was a glimmer in his eyes and he was smiling. I couldn't think of anything to say. He was actually enjoying all this.

It was over as quickly as it had begun.

The plane flew past. The pipes buckled, broke, then fell silent as the pressure went down. Water, suddenly cold, splashed down on the concrete floor. Somewhere in all the steam, McNeil groaned. White and Blondie lay still, their bodies vague outlines in the haze. Powers and I crawled back to the door and stood up. Somehow I found the presence of mind to pick up the mop and bucket. I gave Powers the mop. Together we walked back across the yard. The guards didn't try to stop us.

That night, back in the cell, Powers asked me why I'd saved him.

"I told you." I shrugged, trying to make nothing of it. "I admire you. I wasn't going to let those creeps put a bullet in you."

Powers stood up, holding out a hand. I shook it. "Ya're all right, kid," he said. "Ya're okay."

That was as close as he could get to saying thank you. But I was satisfied as I went to sleep. I'd become his friend, just the way Snape wanted. Surely it could only be a matter of time before I was out of Strangeday Hall.

It was only a matter of time—although things didn't happen quite the way I'd expected. But then, when did they ever?

OUT!

The day after the attack in the shower room, Powers got a letter. We received letters twice a week, but only after the prison warden had censored them. If he didn't like a sentence, he simply took a pair of scissors and cut it out. I got one letter from Tim that more or less fell apart in my hands. It began *Dear Nick,* and ended *Your big brother, Tim.* The rest was just holes apart from the single word "peacock," which I found screwed up at the bottom of the envelope. Well, at least that told me he was still looking for the lost Ming vase. Unless, of course, by some miracle he'd already found it.

The letter Powers got had come through uncut. He read it three times, concentrating on every word. Then he paced up and down the cell for an hour. By now I knew enough not to ask any questions. If Powers wanted me to know something, he would tell me. At last he turned around and walked over to the table. "I'm getting outta here," he said.

"Out, Johnny?" I didn't know what to say. "How come?"

"Read this." He pushed the letter into my hands. I read it.

Johnny,

Bad news, I'm afraid. Grandpa's in emergency care, dear. They're talking of another operation. Kingston Hospital is

ready now, but Grandpa's last operation wasn't very success-
ful. Everyone is really upset.

Caroline and Oliver got married in Edinburgh yesterday.
He's an optician, and marvelous with eyes. We'll all miss them.

No other important news.

Take care.

Yours ever, Ma

I finished the letter and glanced up. Powers was staring at
me, waiting for me to speak. "That's bad," I said.

"Yeah."

"I mean you must be worried about your granddad, but
I don't see—"

"My granddad died ten years ago." He snatched the letter back and spread it out on the table. "Ya don't understand,"
he went on. "Ma and me have this secret code."

I read the letter again, but still couldn't see it.

Powers jerked a thumb toward the page. "Ya take the first
letter of every other word. That way ya get the real message."

I read the letter for a third time, starting with the *B* of
"bad." And at last it made sense.

BIG ED TAKING OVER.
COME HOME AT ONCE.

"Big Ed," I muttered. I'd heard that name only the day before. He'd been the one who'd sent White and the others to
deal with Powers.

"Ya can cut London into four slices," Powers explained. "North, south, east, and west. There's a gang for each slice . . . like, ya know, we got a gentleman's agreement. The east was my territory until I got slammed up here. Since then, my ma's been looking after it. She's an ace, my ma. Top of the world. Now, Big Ed handles the south. That's fine by me. Until he gets greedy. With me outta the way, he thinks maybe he can muscle in on my territory. Only it would be better for him if I was outta the way more permanent like. So he sends White and the others after me. And then he goes gunning after Ma."

Powers paused and I was amazed to see a tear trickle down one of his pale, choirboy cheeks.

"Ya don't know my ma," he said. "She's as tough as old nails. She's a real killer. And her cooking! Nobody makes a moussaka like her—all hot and bubbling with the cheese melted on top. She sent me one here, back in February."

"The St. Valentine's Day moussaka?" I asked.

"That's right. But she can't stand up to Big Ed on her own. She needs me. That's why she sent me the letter."

He got up again and went over to the door. For a minute he listened carefully. When he was satisfied that there was no one there, he came back to the table.

"I'm busting outta here," he said in a low voice. "And ya're coming with me."

"That's terrific!" I said. This is terrible! I thought.

"We'll go together."

"When? How?"

"Ya leave the thinking to me, kid."

And that was all he would say.

Another week passed. I cleaned plates, washed floors, marched around the yard, and fell asleep in class. Powers barely said a word during all this time, but he got two visits from his lawyer. He came back from each visit with a sly, secretive smile and an ugly light in his eyes. Somehow I didn't think they'd been discussing legal niceties. Illegal, more likely, and probably not-very-niceties either.

It all came together one Friday morning, six weeks to the day since my arrival at Strangeday Hall. There were two visiting sessions on Fridays and that morning Powers got a visit—he said it was his cousin. But when he came back into the cell, his face was flushed with excitement.

He waited until he was sure nobody was listening. Then he came over and whispered to me. "It's on," he said. "We go tonight."

"Tonight?"

"That's right, kid. But there's a problem." He pounded his fist into the palm of his hand. "Nails Nathan," he hissed.

"What about him?"

"He's my getaway driver. Only he's sick. He's got food poisoning." Powers kicked the wall. "I'll poison him all right . . ."

"Can't we wait until he gets better?" I asked.

"We can't wait. Everything's been set up. We gotta go tonight." He thought for a minute. "Wait a minute," he said. "Didn't ya say ya brother was visiting ya this afternoon?"

"Yes."

"Can he drive?"

"Yes. But—"

"That's perfect, then." Powers blew on the palm of his hand. "Tell him he's gotta be at Terminal Two—departures, Heathrow, at eleven o'clock tonight."

"Heathrow?" I stared at him. "Are we flying out of here?"

"Ya'll see." Powers gave me another sly smile.

"Just make sure he's there."

"But, Johnny," I stammered. "Tim isn't—"

That was as far as I got. Suddenly the smile was gone and the madness was back in his eyes. "He's ya brother and he can drive. That's all that matters. Don't let me down, kid. I'm counting on ya."

I could have told him that Tim was completely incompetent. I could have told him that he'd only passed his driving test after six attempts and that on the fifth attempt he'd run over the driving instructor. I could have added that Tim was too scared to park on a yellow line, let alone drive a carload of gangsters out of a maximum-security prison. But Johnny Powers was counting on me. If I argued, my number would be up.

"I'll ask him," I said at last.

"Sure, kid. Ask him nicely. And tell him, if he says no"—Powers smiled—"the next drive he'll take will be in a hearse."

The main prison visiting room was long and narrow, divided in half like two mirror reflections. A row of tables ran down the center. Two doors led into the room: one for inmates, one for visitors. The inmates sat at one end of the tables, the visitors at the other. Two guards stood in the room the whole time, listening to every word that was said.

My problem was that I had to tell Tim to be at Heathrow Airport later that night without telling him why. I knew he'd argue—and probably at the top of his voice. And if the guards overheard anything, that would be that.

He was already sitting there, waiting for me, as I came in. He gaped at me like he'd never seen me before. I guessed it was the uniform, the blue denim and stenciled number, that had taken him by surprise. But what had he expected me to be wearing? Top hat and tails? I sat down and for a long time neither of us said anything. Tim loosened his tie and collar.

"It's like a prison in here," he said at last.

"It *is* a prison, Tim," I reminded him.

"Oh yes. Yes, of course." He smiled aimlessly. "How are you?" he asked.

"I'm all right."

"Well—there's only seventeen months to go. And maybe they'll give you time off for good behavior. How is your behavior?"

"It's good," I said.

"Good."

There was a long pause. Tim was obviously lost for words. He'd never had a jailbird for a brother before and of course he still didn't know that I was innocent. He took out a pack of chewing gum and offered it to me.

"No passing food over the table," one of the guards snapped.

"Can I pass it under the table?" Tim asked.

"No food," the guard said.

Tim shrugged, rolled up a piece for himself, and flicked it toward his mouth. It missed and hit him in the eye.

I sighed. "How are Mum and Dad?" I asked.

"I called them in Australia," Tim said. "They didn't take the news very well, I'm afraid. Mum had hysterics. Dad disowned you." There was another long silence. So much for family loyalty.

Tim looked at his watch. "I haven't got long," he said.

"How's the plane spotting going, Tim?" I blurted out.

"The plane spotting?" He looked at me as if I'd gone mad.

"Sure." One of the guards was listening, obviously puzzled. I smiled at him. "Some people spot trains," I said. "My big brother spots planes."

"But—" Tim began.

"Seen any good jumbos lately?" I was smiling frantically now. The guard looked the other way. I winked at Tim. "Didn't you say you were going to Heathrow at eleven o'clock tonight? To the departure lounge in Terminal Two?"

I was still winking furiously. "Have you got something in your eye?" Tim asked.

"That's right." I laughed. "Maybe when you get to Terminal Two at eleven o'clock tonight you can get me some ointment."

"But, Nick . . ."

There was nothing else to do. I stretched under the table and kicked him as hard as I could. Too hard. Tim screamed. Both the guards hurried over to us.

"What's the matter?" one of them asked.

"It's nothing," I said. "My brother was just doing an impersonation. He was taking off a 747. You know . . . a 747 taking off."

"My ankle!" Tim moaned.

"That's right," I continued desperately. "His uncle. He's hurt his uncle by refusing to take him plane spotting at Heathrow tonight."

By now everyone in the room was looking at us. The two guards shook their heads. "Visiting time over," one of them said.

I stood up and followed the other inmates through the door and into the prison. Tim sat where he was, rubbing his ankle and gazing after me. I must have given him quite a bruise. I just hoped he'd gotten the message.

When you're doing time, time passes slowly. But the rest of that afternoon dragged past like a dying man. At last the sun collapsed behind the prison walls and darkness came. Johnny Powers had barely said a word since I'd gotten back from the visiting room. I'd told him that I'd gotten the message across and that Tim would be there.

"Okay, kid. We move at twelve."

He spoke the words without moving his lips and I remember thinking he'd have made a great ventriloquist. And now that he had Tim on the payroll, he wouldn't even need to buy a dummy.

We went down to dinner. I couldn't eat a mouthful. Then it was back into the cells and lockup. Powers dozed off. I lay on my bunk, mentally composing my will. Tim would get my books, my records, and my old stamp collection. I'd leave Snape and Boyle my Australian underpants. *We move at twelve.* How would Powers even know when twelve had arrived? We didn't have a watch. And what was he planning anyway? There were at least four locked doors between us and the main gate. If we climbed the walls we would be too high up to drop down on the other side. And then there were the guards in the watchtowers.

A plane grumbled across the sky. Powers's eyes flickered open.

He didn't say anything. He rolled over and reached underneath the mattress. A moment later he was standing up, the cold moonlight slashing across his face. His eyes were black. There was no color in his skin. The moonlight glinted off the gun he now held in his right hand. The gun from the shower room. He was only fifteen years old but somehow he was already dead. A discarded frame from one of those old black-and-white gangster films.

He turned to me.

"It's twelve o'clock, kid," he said. "Time to go."

OVER THE WALL

"What do we do, Johnny?"

"Get on ya bunk. Put ya hands on ya stomach. And start groaning," he said.

I hesitated for about half a second. Just long enough for him to turn around and hiss, "Move it!" Then I clambered up, curled into a ball, and began to groan like I was about to throw up. Which, in fact, I was. I always feel a little queasy when I'm afraid and right then I was scared out of my mind.

Powers glanced back at me, winked, and began to hammer on the door. I could hear the sound echoing down the corridors. There were heavy footsteps on the catwalk, coming our way.

"Guard!" Powers shouted. "Guard!" One of the other prisoners yelled something out. Then there was a rattle of keys and the door swung open. I groaned louder. Powers took a step back.

Walsh was on duty that night. I could just see him out of the corner of my eye, framed in the soft, yellow light of the doorway. "What's the matter, 00666?" he asked.

"It's the kid," Powers said. "He's sick."

After the shower-room affair, Walsh didn't trust either of

us. I thought for a moment he was going to walk away. I gave
a ghastly croak and shuddered. It wouldn't have won me any
major acting awards, but it seemed to convince Walsh. He
walked past Powers, farther into the cell, and stood beside me.
Powers made a sign at me as he edged toward the door. The
meaning was clear. Keep Walsh talking.

"I'm sick," I groaned. "I need a doctor."

"What's the matter with you?"

"I don't know. That's why I need the doctor."

"You look okay to me." Walsh was suspicious.

"Yeah—but you're not a doctor," I pointed out.

Meanwhile, Johnny had looked up and down the corridor,
checking that there was no one else around. As Walsh
straightened up, he moved. Suddenly the gun was pressed
against his neck and Powers was right up close to him,
purring like a kitten. A rabid kitten.

"Weasel Walsh," he muttered. "Make one false move and
I'll decorate the walls with ya brains."

"Powers!" The color had drained out of Walsh's face. "Are
you crazy?"

"Sure." Powers laughed. "That's what my doctors say.
But I ain't so crazy about this joint, Walsh. That's why ya're
going to be my ticket out." He jerked his head toward the
door. "Check it again, kid," he said. I went over and looked
out. The narrow corridor seemed to stretch into infinity, the
dull yellow bulbs throwing sticky pools of light onto the floor.

"It's clear, Johnny," I said.

"Let's go!" Powers pushed Walsh toward me. "Ya try anything Walsh and it's pop goes the weasel."

We stepped into the corridor. It's a strange thing about prison. After a while you get used to being locked up. To me it felt all wrong being outside the cell in the middle of the night. The shadows seemed to reach out as if to grab me. Everything was somehow too big. I could hear my heart pulsing in my ears and the hair on my forehead was damp with sweat. I wanted to go back. I wanted to hear the cell door slam shut behind me. Now I knew what our hamster must have felt like when it went AWOL one Christmas.

Four doors stood between us and the main gate. Walsh had opened the first three without any problem. But as he turned the key in the fourth, the sirens screamed and the whole world went crazy.

We'd climbed a flight of stairs and we were high up. We were also outside. The cold night air came at me in a rush. The sirens were everywhere, ripping into the night. Somebody switched on a spotlight. I saw a perfect circle of light glide across the courtyard far below us then ripple along the wall, counting the bricks. Then it hit us. For a horrible moment I was completely blind. It was a brilliant, exploding blindness. I thought I was going to fall, but Powers must have reached out and grabbed me because I felt myself pulled back, my shoulders slamming into the wall behind me.

The fourth door led nowhere. We were on a small

platform, about thirty feet above the ground, the same height as the wall. The platform was directly opposite one of the watchtowers. I could just make out the shape of two guards behind the curtain of light. They were pointing something at us—something long and thin. Somehow I didn't think it was a telescope. Sitting ducks. I waited for the crackle of gunfire that would bring it all to an end.

But it didn't come. Instead the sirens ended, abruptly fading into silence. Now I could hear people shouting. About half a dozen guards ran into the yard, making for the shadows. I looked at Powers. Did he have any idea how he was going to get us out of here? He'd told me to tell Tim to go to Heathrow. I gazed up at the sky almost expecting to see a helicopter—but that was insane. Powers wanted a driver, not a pilot. So what happened next?

"Listen to me!" Powers shouted. "Do what I tell ya and nobody gets hurt."

"Put down the gun and give yourself up, Powers." I don't know who said that. It was just a voice out of the darkness.

"I got nothing to lose," Powers called back. "If I don't get some action, Walsh here takes a dive." He pushed Walsh to the very edge of the platform. I had to admit, he knew what he was doing. If anybody took a potshot at him now, the guard would fall. "Lower the drawbridge," Powers yelled. "Do it now!"

I'd forgotten the drawbridge. Each watchtower was connected to the prison by a strip of metal that could be lowered or raised automatically. That was why Powers had taken us up and not down into the yard. But would they lower it for him? I'd no sooner asked myself that than there was a low hum and a rectangular shape pushed through the spotlight toward me. So long as Powers held Walsh, he held all the cards.

The drawbridge connected with the platform and the way ahead was clear. I looked at Powers. He was grinning from ear to ear like a kid at a carnival.

"All right," he shouted at the two guards in the watchtower. "Drop ya weapons and come over here. But slowly. And no tricks."

The guards did as they were told, and half a minute later there were five of us up there, crowded together in the narrow space.

"You'll never get away with this, Powers," one of them said.

"No? Just watch me. Come on, kid . . ."

Well, I suppose it was nice that somebody had remembered me. Up to now it had been as if nobody had noticed that I was escaping, too. Holding Walsh between us, Powers and I shuffled over to the watchtower and went inside.

"Raise it!" Powers hissed.

Walsh reached out and flicked a switch. The drawbridge swung up again.

So there we now were, cut off in the watchtower with the wall right beside us and a window leading out. But we were still in the prison. If we jumped from the window we'd be lucky to escape with just a broken leg. We wouldn't escape at all. It was a thirty-foot drop and the road running alongside the prison was one hundred percent concrete.

"You can't get down from here, Powers," Walsh said, echoing my thoughts exactly.

"Ya think so?" Powers glanced in my direction. "See anything, kid?"

I looked back out of the window. And there was something. I'd never seen anything like it. It wasn't a car. It wasn't a truck. It was a long rectangular box, riding some twelve feet above the ground. It was held up on hydraulic arms, the wheels far below. Four mattresses had been strapped to the roof. It was driving down the road at about fifteen miles an hour. And it was coming toward us.

"It's coming, Johnny," I said—even though I didn't know what "it" was.

"Here's something to remember me by, Weasel," Powers snarled. He'd turned the gun around in his hand, and before either of us could react he brought it crashing down. Walsh crumpled. I was relieved to see that he was still breathing. I'd never liked him much, but he was just an ordinary man doing his job. I went back to the window. The platform was getting closer.

"We jump?" I asked.

We climbed out of the window and hung there awkwardly. There was no sound from inside the prison. Nobody could see us. Perhaps they didn't realize what we were about to do. The truck or whatever it was veered toward us without slowing down. Close up, it seemed to be going much faster than I'd thought and whoever was driving it clearly wasn't too sure of himself. It was wobbling all over the place, the tires thumping into the curb. At one point it swerved away and I was afraid it was going to miss us altogether. But then it veered back again.

"Now!" Powers shouted.

We dropped.

It was still a long way to fall. It felt like I was in midair forever, like Alice on her way to Wonderland. I heard the engine roaring in my ears. Then I hit the mattress, rolled over, scrabbled for a handhold, somehow managed to cling on. It was a heavy landing. I didn't break any bones, but I must have broken a few springs.

Powers was beside me. "Move inside," he said.

The platform was still zigzagging down the road. Not exactly breakneck speed, unless, that is, you fell off. It was still a long way to fall. With the wind blowing in my hair, I crawled along the roof to the back end. There was a square opening beneath me and I could see lights inside. The wheels hit the curb again, sending a garbage can flying. Gritting my teeth, I grabbed hold of the edge and heaved myself into space. Now I was hanging there with the road sweeping away behind me. I tried to swing into the box. Then a strong pair of hands reached out and took hold of me. I was pulled inside, dropping the last couple of feet onto the floor. I stood up and blinked. And only then did I realize what kind of getaway vehicle we were getting away in.

If you've ever been to an airport you may have seen them. They're called "people movers" or something like that. Imagine an ordinary airport bus, only with more seats and bright neon lights. Then put metal arms between the wheels and the undercarriage. When you step out of the plane, you're about twelve feet off the ground. But you don't need steps. The driver simply parks the people mover beside the plane, presses a button, and the whole thing rises into the air until it's level with the door. You step inside. The bus sinks back down onto the wheels. And you speed away to the arrival lounge, where, provided your driver isn't Tim Diamond, you finally arrive.

But our driver *was* Tim. I could see him at the far end of the bus, sitting in a sort of miniature cubicle, surrounded by switches and levers. He was making the most peculiar noises, whimpering and squeaking with every turn of the wheel.

"Johnny boy!" a voice said behind me.

I turned around. Powers had followed me into the people mover and now he was gazing at the man who had pulled us in. Only it wasn't a man. It was a woman. And I didn't need to ask her name to know who she was.

Ma Powers. Johnny's mother.

On first sight she was like any other mother. She was about fifty, wearing a severe black skirt, a matching jacket, and a flowery shirt buttoned at the neck. Her hair was gray, mainly hidden by a black velvet hat. Her only makeup was a dash of red lipstick across her tight-lipped mouth. For jewelry she wore plain gold earrings and a cameo brooch in the shape of a rose.

But *un*like any other mother, she was carrying a submachine gun, the barrel slanting across her chest. The more I looked at her, the less I liked her. Her eyes—like Johnny's—were two bullet holes in a refrigerator door. She had a tough, weathered face, and when I say weathered I'm talking storms and blizzards. Her skin was as tough as leather. Her teeth when she smiled, which wasn't often, were yellow and crammed together uncomfortably like being in a subway during rush hour.

"How ya doing, Johnny?" she asked. She spoke just like him, only her voice was deeper.

"I'm okay, Ma," Powers said. "All the better for seeing you."

"That ya friend?" She nodded at me.

"That's right, Ma. Nick . . . come and meet my ma."

"Not now, Johnny boy. We gotta move."

Even as she spoke, I heard the scream of approaching police cars. Looking through the open end of the bus, I could see the flash of blue lights in the distance. Tim groaned. We were still only doing twenty miles an hour. At that speed, they'd catch up with us in seconds.

"Go and check with ya brother," Ma Powers commanded.

"I'll hold 'em off." She cocked the machine gun and moved to the back.

"Has Nails fixed the bus?" Powers asked.

"Sure, Johnny boy. Bulletproof windows. Sawed-off back. And a souped-up engine." She glared at me. "Shame we ain't got a souped-up driver. Tell him to put his foot down."

Powers and I ran up to the front of the bus. Tim was white-faced, his eyes staring, his hands clutching the steering wheel like he was trying to pull it apart.

"Nick . . . !" he began when he saw me.

"Not now, Tim," I said.

"Can't ya lower this thing?" Powers rasped. We were still twelve feet off the ground, higher than the top deck of a London bus. Only there was no bottom deck.

"I don't know how it works," Tim whimpered.

"Didn't Ma show ya?"

"Yes. But I've forgotten."

"Take the next turn on the left!" Ma Powers called out.

Tim put his foot down and swung the wheel to the left. The people mover surged forward with fresh power, skidding around the corner. For a horrible moment we were driving on two wheels and I thought the whole thing would topple over. But then it somehow managed to right itself.

"Lower the bus!" Ma Powers shouted.

"Lower the bus!" I screamed.

I'd seen it the moment we'd turned the corner. A road sign

in a red triangle: LOW BRIDGE AHEAD, CLEARANCE NINE FEET. About three feet too low. Tim had seen it, too. He took his foot off the accelerator and at once we slowed down. There was a chatter of machine-gun fire from the back of the bus.

"Keep moving!" Ma Powers yelled.

She was cradling the machine gun like a bouquet of flowers. Except that I've never seen a bouquet with smoke curling out of the end. Looking past her, I saw that the first of the police cars had reached the turn. Despite our souped-up engine, it was gaining on us. And there were four more right behind it.

"What do I do?" Tim moaned.

"Just keep going—fast," Powers said. Tim was about to argue, but there was something in Johnny's tone of voice that made him think again. He gave a little squeak and stomped down on the accelerator. We rocketed forward.

The machine gun chattered again. The road was narrow now, hemmed in on both sides by a wire fence. There was only one way to go and that was straight ahead. But there was the bridge. It was looming up at us, a humpback bridge with a railway line on top. I could see the rails. I was actually looking down at them. At the rate we were going, we would hit it in around thirty seconds. The metal box of the people mover would crash right into the brickwork. I didn't like to think what would happen to the people inside.

Powers ran back to join his mother—perhaps to warn her. I stood beside Tim, fighting to keep my balance as we bounced over the tarmac, hurtling toward the bridge. He wasn't even trying to lower the bus. He was too frightened to let go of the steering wheel. Desperately I examined the controls. Why did there have to be so many levers? Ma Powers fired for the third time. And this time she found her target. The siren of the nearest police car died away. There was a screech of tires, a shattering of metal, then an explosion. The bridge glowed red. Twenty seconds until impact.

I ran my hands over the controls, frantically flicking switches and pulling levers left, right, and center. I turned out the lights, opened and closed the doors, lowered the antenna, and adjusted the mirrors. But I didn't lower the bus. Behind us, Powers was shooting with the pistol he'd taken from the prison. Mother and son seemed to be having a whale of a time. A second police car had moved up to take the position of the first. And now they were firing, too. I tugged at another lever. The ashtray popped out of the dashboard. Ten seconds until impact.

The bridge was right in front of me now, filling up the windshield. Tim was whispering something. I think it was a prayer. I slammed my hand down on the controls. My palm hit the black ball at the end of the lever, shifting it forward. I heard a hiss underneath me. The hydraulic arm had come into operation. At the same moment, the whole bus began to sink like the end of a ride in a carnival.

But would it sink in time? There were only a few seconds left.

"Brake, Tim!" I shouted.

We hit the bridge.

We were just low enough to squeeze through. In fact, the mattresses didn't make it. I heard them as they were torn free from their bindings and dragged along the roof. Looking back, I saw them plummet into the road behind us, right in the path of the leading police car. It swerved to avoid them, mounted the curb, and crashed through the fence, finally crushing itself against a lamppost. Ma Powers gave a short bray of laughter.

"Good work, kid," Johnny called out.

But it wasn't over yet. We'd taken out two of the five police cars. That still left three and already they were moving up on us. Ma Powers let off a hail of bullets. I heard a windshield shatter but they kept on coming. Two of them surged ahead. One stayed behind to keep the back of the bus covered.

The road was wider now. The two police cars had edged forward and separated, so there was one on each side, with us sandwiched in the middle.

"Nick . . ." Tim muttered.

There wasn't much traffic about at that time of night, but looking ahead, I saw a truck thundering toward us. But with the two police cars on either side, we were taking up all the road. Somebody would have to give.

The truck gave. At the last second, with its headlights dazzling us and the blast of its horn deafening us, it swerved away, left the road, and jackknifed into a field. The truck had been carrying eggs. I know because some of them splattered into our windshield. With the horn still blaring, the truck hit a tree stump, somersaulted, and burst into flames. Later I heard that nobody had been killed. But between us we'd cooked up a fifty-thousand-egg omelette.

We were doing nearly seventy miles an hour by now. Ahead of us, cars were vacating the road as fast as they could—and they didn't seem to care where they ended up. But they weren't our problem. We were down at ground level. The two police cars were only inches away, racing alongside us. They had rolled down their windows. Two shotguns were pointing at us, one on each side. Two blasts and Tim and I would have more holes than a colander. We couldn't slow down, not with the third police car behind us. We were going as fast as we could. We were stuck.

I stared at the nearest policeman, watched his finger tighten on the trigger. For a moment our eyes met and we were trapped in a blue-and-white nightmare. There was nothing I could do.

Nothing? At the last second I slammed my hand down on the controls. The bus rose into the air again. Simultaneously, the two shotguns fired. But now we were above them. The bullets passed underneath us. The police car on the left hit the one on the right. The police car on the right shredded the tires of the one on the left. Both cars went careering off in opposite directions.

Four down. One to go.

But it seemed that I'd pushed the lever a little too hard. Something had shortcircuited. We were no sooner up at the end of the hydraulic arms than we were on the way down again. And that was how we continued, up and down like some crazy jack-in-the-box.

"What are ya doing?" Powers called out.

"It's broken," Tim cried.

That was the understatement of the year. Sparks were flashing all over the control box. There was a smell of burning rubber and a wisp of smoke crawled into the air. Up and down. I could feel my stomach protesting. It was trying to go the other way.

Then the fifth police car pulled out and began to overtake us. It was the last one left and perhaps the driver thought he could cut us off. Ma Powers opened her handbag, pulled out a spare cartridge, and reloaded the machine gun. Johnny followed her as she staggered forward to get a better aim. The control box was on fire now. The engine was howling at us to stop. The hydraulic arms were creaking and shuddering as they pumped us madly up and down. I reckoned we had only a few minutes left before the whole thing either broke down or blew up.

Those last few minutes happened very quickly.

One moment we were up. The next we were at the same level as the police car. It was edging ahead, about to overtake us. Ma Powers raised the machine gun. Then I saw the two passengers in the backseat.

"No!" I shouted.

It was Snape and Boyle. I had no idea what they were doing there but it was definitely them. I could even swear that Snape winked at me before Ma Powers opened fire. But I was still shouting when the machine gun drowned me out. I saw the windows of Snape's car frost over in a thousand cracks. I saw the tires cut to ribbons. I saw the mirrors and door handles spin away into the night. The car veered into us, out of control, then swung away. I watched it spiral into the curb. Then it was as if somebody had picked it up and thrown it. It took off, bounced, then cartwheeled into a telephone booth. A few seconds later it exploded.

They were dead. Snape and Boyle were dead. There was no way they could have survived. And they were the only people in the world who knew that I'd been framed. They were my only way out of this mess. And they were dead.

I could have cried. But I didn't have time.

There was a sharp bend in the road. I heard Tim cry out. I looked up. He was spinning the wheel desperately. But we were going too fast. He'd lost control. Ma Powers dropped the machine gun. Johnny swore. The people mover, at ground level, left the road, sliced through a hedge, and hurtled toward a building. Tim didn't even have time to slam on the brakes. Traveling at seventy miles an hour, we smashed into the wall.

At least, the wheels did. But by the time the impact came, the hydraulic arms had lifted us up again. The wheels, the engine, and the undercarriage flattened themselves against solid brick. But the bus itself was twelve feet up, the same height as the first floor. And on the first floor there was a plate-glass window.

The force of the impact tore the bus off the hydraulic arms. As the gas tank ignited and the undercarriage erupted in flames, the bus itself came free, rammed itself through the window, and slid along the floor of the building. The place was an empty office building. There was nothing inside to stop our progress. Carried by our own velocity, we slid the full length of the floor, and then, with another explosion of breaking glass—exited through a second window on the other side.

This is it, I muttered to myself as we rocketed out. *Now we've got to die.*

But the office building looked out over the River Thames. We landed, not with a crash but a splash. And when I finally found the courage to open my eyes, we were floating gently on the water. We were bruised, shaken, and exhausted. But we were still alive.

We floated the rest of the way. There were roadblocks all over London, but we sailed right past them. Nobody had thought to contact the river police. I was free. Over the wall. But Snape and Boyle were dead.

So what did I do next?

WAPPING LIES

It's funny how often the River Thames seems to feature in my life. Once, I was locked up beside it and almost drowned in it. The next time you take a pleasure boat down from Charing Cross pier, look out for a kid dressed in jeans and a baggy sweater floating facedown in the dirty water. It'll probably be me.

The river took us all the way to Wapping. It's just as well the tide was going in our direction or we'd have been out of London via Windsor and on our way to Wales. Even so it was quite a journey. Under Vauxhall Bridge and down past the Houses of Parliament, Somerset House, and the National Theatre. Then around the corner and on past Traitor's Gate and the Tower of London, the redeveloped St. Katharine's Dock, and almost as far as the Isle of Dogs.

This was East London, the heart of Johnny's criminal empire. And looking at it in the cold half-light of the early morning, he was welcome to it.

Everything was gray: the sky, the water, the broken hulks of the old barges moored along the banks. The south side of the river was long and flat, punctuated by a tangle of cranes here, a gas pile there, in the distance a forlorn church steeple.

We moored on the north side at a jetty between two warehouses. There was nobody around. There had probably been nobody in those warehouses for fifty years. A derelict houseboat stood firm a few yards away, tied to the bank and somehow resisting the chop and swell of the Thames water. Shivering, we pulled ourselves out of the broken people mover and stood on damp—if not quite dry—land.

"Where do we go now?" I asked.

"Home," Ma Powers said. Her lips were set in a frigid scowl. Either it was the cold or she didn't like me. Possibly both.

"East London," I muttered. "I'd have thought that was the first place the police would expect us to go."

"Sure." Johnny slapped me on the back. "So it's the last place they'll come looking."

With Tim bringing up the rear, we hurried off the jetty and between the warehouses to Wapping High Street. And if this was the high street, I'd hate to see what the low street looked like. It was a spiderweb of rusting metal with cranes and scaffolding everywhere. Half the buildings had fallen down. Half of them had only been half built. It was hard to tell which was which. A patchwork of corrugated iron filled in the gaps, old posters clinging on with tattered fingers. There were no pavements. You couldn't see where the road ended and the gutter began.

We passed through the wreckage and reached another road running off at a right angle. There was a barrier across it with a big sign in red and white: ROAD CLOSED. It was blocked by a slanting wall of scaffolding holding up a row of dirty, decrepit houses. We stopped beside the fourth house. Ma Powers fumbled in her handbag and pulled out a set of keys. She turned one in the lock and we went in. We were home.

Johnny Powers needed somewhere to hole up for a while and he'd chosen a real hole. The house was three stories high, only the third story had collapsed in on itself. The ground floor was one big room with a couch, a table and chairs, a TV set, and an open-plan kitchen. It had been a closed-plan kitchen until the dividing wall had fallen over. Two doors led out—one to a toilet, the other to a bedroom. There were two more bedrooms and a bathroom upstairs. You could see the bath through a hole in the ceiling.

"Home sweet home," I muttered.

"It's safe," Ma Powers said.

"Safe?" I tapped the mantelpiece. A chunk of it fell off. "You could have fooled me."

"The police won't come looking for us here," Johnny said. "That's what Ma means."

"What about the neighbors?"

"There are no neighbors," Ma Powers growled. "All the houses are condemned."

"Yeah—and sentenced and executed, too," I said.

Johnny turned to his mother and smiled. "Ya made it real nice, Ma," he purred.

I suppose she had done her best to make it comfortable. There were fresh flowers on the table and homemade cushions on the couch. A circular rug lay on the floor, a few pictures hung on the walls, and she'd covered the windows with net curtains. But it was like rearranging the cutlery after the *Titanic* had gone down. The whole place was a disaster. Dry rot, rising damp, termites, mold . . . the building would have given a surveyor a field day. Sneeze, and a field would be all that was left.

The door to the bedroom opened and another guy walked in. He was about the same age as Johnny, thin and with so much acne you could have struck a match on him. This had to be Nails Nathan. He was biting them even as he walked in. In fact, he'd bitten them so far down that he'd started on the fingers. Another few months and they'd have to rechristen him Knuckles Nathan.

"So you made it, Johnny," he said, smiling nervously and blinking.

"Sure I made it." Johnny advanced on him. "But no thanks to you, ya sap."

"I'm sorry, Johnny." Nails was whining now. He ran his teeth down the side of his thumb and bit at his wrist. "I was sick. I couldn't drive." He paused hopefully. "But I fixed the car up for you. I did that."

"You did good, kid." Johnny gave him a friendly punch in the stomach. Nails doubled up. "Now fix us some breakfast. And make sure the coffee's good and strong."

Tim had been watching all this standing beside the front door. He hadn't said a word, which was probably the best thing he could have done. But now he sort of staggered forward and sat down heavily at the table. So heavily that another chunk fell off the mantelpiece.

"I don't believe this," he said.

"Who is this guy, Johnny boy?" Ma Powers demanded. She was propping up the machine gun in the corner like it was a walking stick and she'd just come back from an amble in the park. "I met him at the airport like ya told me, but I couldn't get no sense outta him. He went on . . . something about plane spotting."

Johnny laughed and began to roll himself a cigarette. "Ma," he said, "ya ain't met my friend Nick Diamond. He saved my life back in the slammer. That's his big brother Tim."

"Tim?" Ma Powers looked at him suspiciously. "What do you do for a living, Tim?"

"I'm a private investigator," Tim said.

There was a long silence. Nails Nathan dropped a plate. Johnny stared. Right then you could have cut the atmosphere with a knife. Right then I could have cut Tim with a knife. Why did he have to go and tell them that? Why couldn't he say he was a certified public accountant or a postman or a brain surgeon or something? Snape had told me that Johnny Powers hated policemen. I somehow guessed he wasn't exactly wild about detectives either.

"A private investigator?" he repeated, narrowing his eyes.

"That's right," I cut in quick before anyone could say another word. "Tim investigates"—Nails had turned on a tap to fill the kettle and it was still running—"water! He's a private investigator of water."

"What is there to investigate about water?" Ma Powers demanded.

"All sorts of things," I said. "The amount of chlorine. The bacteria. The . . . um . . . the H."

"The H?"

"Yeah—you know. Water is H_2O. Tim has to make sure there's enough H. He works for the Thames Water Authority."

"Okay." Ma Powers shook her head slowly. "Maybe that explains why he's such a drip."

The ice had been broken—or at least, the water. Nails laid the table and we sat down to a breakfast of bacon sandwiches, strong coffee, shredded wheat, and grapefruit yogurt. The last two had been suggested by Ma Powers. Without the machine gun she was just like anyone's mother. I think I preferred her with it.

"Ya don't look so good, Johnny boy," she said. "Did ya eat proper food in prison?"

"Sure, Ma . . ."

"Plenny of fruit? Here—have some grapefruit yogurt."

"I'm okay, Ma . . ."

"Do ya want Mummy to get ya some sugar?"

"Ma . . ."

"Yogurt's good for you, Johnny," Nails chipped in, spooning out some of his own.

He should have kept his mouth shut. Johnny suddenly picked up his plastic container and slammed it into Nathan's face, crumpling it against his cheek. Grapefruit yogurt dripped over his chin and onto his shirt. Ma Powers raised her eyebrows but said nothing. Tim sighed and reached for the shredded wheat. He wasn't looking too good. I guess his nerves were pretty shredded, too.

But at least Johnny cheered up a few minutes later when he finished his coffee and turned on the television. Breakfast TV had just started and the first thing he saw was his own face, a police mug shot taken a few months before.

". . . a daring escape from Strangeday Hall late last night. Powers, who was serving fifteen years for armed robbery, is described by the police as unpredictable and extremely dangerous. The public is warned not to approach him."

The picture flickered off to be replaced by the newscaster. He was looking out of the screen with tired eyes, trying not to yawn.

"Accompanying Powers in the breakout was a thirteen-year-old known as Nicholas Diamond . . ."

And there I was suddenly on TV. It was the same photograph that had appeared in all the newspapers. Young, innocent, smiling . . . you couldn't believe all the things the newscaster was saying about me.

"Diamond, arrested only a month ago following the

brutal Woburn Carbuncle robbery, is described as violent and ruthless. In fact, if Johnny Powers is Public Enemy Number One, Diamond must now be considered Public Enemy Number Two.

"Police are still looking for Tim Diamond, Nicholas's elder brother, who may be able to help them with their inquiries."

Johnny switched off the set.

"They're looking for me!" Tim moaned. He was staring at the blank screen as if the newscaster was about to climb out and grab him.

"Of course they're looking for ya." Johnny grinned at me. "Public Enemy Number Two! Ya moved up in the charts pretty quick—eh, kid?"

"Yeah." I tried to look delighted. It wasn't easy. "What happens next, Johnny?"

"Right now ya get some sleep. I reckon we could all do with some shut-eye. Isn't that right, Ma?"

"That's right, Johnny boy."

"Meantime, Nails can go out and get the rest of the boys together. I'll see them at four. So, Nails . . . ya better get a box of cupcakes or something."

"Sure thing, Johnny."

"Good." Johnny patted me on the shoulder. "Public Enemy Number Two? I like that, kid. It suits ya."

At last Tim and I were alone.

We were sharing a bedroom on the second floor. It was

about as comfortable as the living room. There were two single beds leaning unsteadily toward each other, a chair with three legs, and a wardrobe minus the door. The window looked out onto a construction site behind the house, only there was so much dirt on the glass you could barely see anything.

For a long time neither of us said anything. Tim looked exhausted. His face was streaked with dust and his hair was standing on end.

"How could you do it, Nick?" he said at last. "My own brother! First the robbery . . . and then this. I mean . . . this Johnny Flowers. He's insanely criminal. I mean, he's criminally insane. And his mother! How could you do it? I'm wanted by the police! When they find me it'll be the end. They'll lock me up. I'll never find the Purple Peacock. I won't ever get another job. They'll probably give me twenty years, Nick. Twenty years! That's not to be sneezed at . . ." He pounded his fist into the pillow. Dust rose in a cloud and he sneezed loudly.

"Listen," I said. "I didn't do it, Tim. I never stole the carbuncle."

"But, Nick. The judge—"

"I was framed, Tim. I didn't know it at the time— although maybe I should have guessed . . ."

Slowly I explained everything that had happened. The visit from Snape and Boyle, the Fence, Woburn Abbey, Johnny Powers. Then I explained it again using words with fewer syllables. It took me about twenty minutes and all the time Tim sat there, grasping the mattress.

I wasn't sure he'd grasped anything else. But when I finally stopped he stared at me and scratched his head.

"You mean . . . you didn't do it?" he said.

"That's what I've been trying to tell you, Tim."

"And the only people who know are Snape and Boyle? But Snape and Boyle . . ."

"Yeah. They bought it."

"They bought the carbuncle?"

"No. They crashed. They're dead."

"So what do we do now?"

I stood up and went over to the door. "I don't know," I admitted. "I suppose the only thing we can do is try to track down this Fence that everyone wants. If the police ever catch up with us, it might be something to bargain with. But in the meantime . . ." I swung around on Tim. "You've got to convince Johnny and Ma Powers that you're a real crook. If they ever find out you're a private eye, it'll be curtains for us."

Tim glanced at the window "This place could do with some curtains," he said.

"They'll kill us, Tim! I mean *really* kill us. You've got to think like a gangster. Act like a gangster. Be a gangster. And you've got to start now."

Tim got to his feet and straightened his shoulders, drawing his hands across his chest. He gave me an ugly sneer and threw back his head. "I'm Al Capone," he growled.

"Al Ka-seltzer more like," I muttered, but I don't think he heard me.

I left him there and went into the bathroom. I meant to wash up before I turned in. And that was where I had my first big break of the day. I'd turned on the tap and watched it cough out a trickle of brown sludge when I heard a door open underneath me. Quickly I turned it off again. I've mentioned that you could see the bath from the living room through a hole in the ceiling. Well, the same hole allowed me to eavesdrop on a conversation between Ma Powers and her son. And they thought they were alone.

"Your headache gone, Johnny boy?" she was saying.

"Yeah, Ma. Ya made it better for me."

"Ya gonna be okay when the gang gets here?"

"I'm gonna be just fine."

"Ya gotta show them who's boss around here, Johnny boy. With Big Ed trying to move in on you—"

"I got plans for Big Ed, Ma."

I knelt down and peeped through the hole. From that angle I could just make out the back of Johnny's head. Ma Powers was somewhere out of my vision. That was just as well. If I couldn't see her, she couldn't see me.

"First we're gonna do a raid," Johnny went on. "Something really big . . . ya know, to put myself back on the map. Maybe the Bank of England or the Crown Jewels. I don't know. Then I'm gonna go gunning for Big Ed."

"Ya'll need guns, Johnny."

"Sure, Ma. That's why I'm gonna see the Fence later today—before the meeting."

My ears pricked up at that. It seemed almost too good to be true. And what Ma Powers said next was even better.

"So ya're going to Penelope?" she asked.

"That's right. I'll buy enough guns to start a war."

"Then ya'd better get some sleep, Johnny. I don't want my boy starting no war with bags under his eyes."

"Ya're good to me, Ma."

"I love ya, Johnny."

They went back into the bedroom after that and I heard no more. But as I straightened up and went back into my own bedroom, I was feeling better than I'd felt in a long, long time. Snape and Boyle might be dead. I might be wanted by the police. But at last I knew something about the Fence.

He wasn't a man. He was a woman. And the woman's name was Penelope.

VANISHING ACT

Tim woke me up six hours later, in time for lunch. I opened my eyes, then shut them again. Taking a deep breath, I opened them for a second time. I groaned. I really was seeing what I thought I was seeing. And I still couldn't believe it.

I'd told Tim to act like a gangster. He'd taken me at my word and found a costume to match. He had changed into an old-fashioned gray suit, double-breasted with buttons running down both sides, a white shirt, and a narrow tie. There was a hat to match, a soft one with a band running all the way around. It was pulled low over his eyes. So low he could barely see. A handkerchief poking out of his top pocket almost completed the picture. All that was missing was a machine gun in a violin case.

"Wake up, kid," he drawled out of the corner of his mouth. "This is Big Tim talking."

"Tim . . ." I mumbled. "Where did you get that suit?"

"I found it in the wardrobe. There are plenty of clothes for you. So let's move. It's time to eat."

I opened my mouth to call him back but he'd already gone. Hastily I dressed in a fresh shirt but the same trousers and shoes that I'd worn at Strangeday Hall. Then I went back downstairs and into the main room.

I'd wondered what Johnny and his mother would make of Tim's performance and now I saw. They were in shock. Ma Powers had cooked some spaghetti and Johnny and Nails Nathan were both eating. But every now and then they glanced at Tim—"Big Tim," as he called himself—and shook their heads in disbelief.

Johnny threw down his fork. "I gotta go out," he said. He glanced at Tim. "Your brother okay, kid?" he asked.

"Sure, Johnny," I said. "He's just a bit overexcited."

"Maybe ya'd better look after him."

"I'll do that, Johnny."

He stood up and touched the back of his hand briefly against his mother's cheek.

"Make sure ya get back in time for the meeting, Johnny boy," she said.

"That's right, Johnny boy," Tim agreed.

Johnny's eyes were suddenly cold, but he kept himself under control. "I'll be back in a couple of hours," he said. "Nobody leaves the house until I get back. Ya got that?"

He went into the downstairs bedroom to put on a coat. At the same time I grabbed Tim and hurried back up to our room.

As soon as we were in, I went over to the window and opened it.

"What are you doing?" Tim asked.

"I'm going," I said. "Johnny's got an appointment with the Fence and I mean to be there."

"How do you know?"

"I'll tell you later." I swung a leg over the windowsill. "Cover for me until I get back."

"What shall I tell them?"

"Tell them I've gone back to sleep."

"But what if they find you gone?"

"I don't know." I shrugged. "Tell them I've gone out for a walk."

I pulled myself over the ledge and looked around me, trying to find a way down. That wasn't difficult. The window wasn't that high up to start with and there was a pile of rubble climbing halfway up the wall. I let go and dropped on all fours . . . as quiet as a cat. Actually I landed on a cat. It screeched and howled then shot away. So much for stealth! Johnny Powers would have heard it all on the other side of the river.

I crouched for a minute breathing heavily, wondering if anyone would come and look. If they found me there, I'd tell them I'd fallen out of bed. But nobody came. My luck was holding out. It must have been a black cat I'd landed on.

I hurried around the backs of the houses trying not to turn over too many loose bricks with my feet. I heard a door open and close at the front of the house.

"See ya, Ma."

"Look after yaself, Johnny boy."

As I reached the end of the terrace, Johnny Powers walked into sight, making steady progress toward the river. I ducked back around the corner and waited, my shoulders pressed against the brick until he passed. I let him get a short way ahead. Then I followed.

He reached Wapping High Street and turned right. I let him turn a corner before I ran on. This was a Saturday and the road was deserted, the construction sites still empty. On the one hand that was good news. With my face on TV and doubtless back in the papers, I didn't want to be seen by any passersby. But on the other hand, it made it doubly difficult to follow Powers without being spotted by him. If he turned around there would be no one between us, no crowd for me to melt into. Apart from a few cars parked along the side of the road—as ancient and as dusty as the buildings themselves—there was no cover.

I reached the corner just in time to see Powers walk into a subway station—Wapping Station on the East London Line. What did I do now? I didn't have any money on me, so I couldn't buy a ticket, and anyway someone would be sure to recognize me in the crowded subway. But that was also true of him. The more I thought about it, the crazier it seemed. Powers was Public Enemy Number One. He couldn't just get on a train with a return ticket to the West End.

I didn't think about it long. I'd come this far and I wasn't going to give up now. Maybe he was meeting this Penelope woman on the platform. Maybe there was an exit leading to the river on the other side.

There was a small kiosk on the right but with no one in it. The way down to the platforms was on the other side. I slipped past quickly without being stopped. And now I could hear Johnny Powers, walking ahead of me, his footsteps echoing upward. A staircase led down into the gloom and there were also two elevators. I thought of taking one of them, but that would have meant arriving ahead of him. If he doubled back, I would miss him. I made for the stairs.

A central shaft plummeted downward with the concrete staircase sweeping around the edge in a great curve. The walls were white, the paint blistered and flaking. The air was cold and dank, carrying with it the smell of the Thames. And yet in the middle, the elevators, bright red and modern, soared smoothly up and down. They were time capsules. The rest of the station had gotten stuck in the Victorian age.

From above, I saw Johnny Powers head off for the southbound platform. So he was planning to travel away from the center of London—over to Rotherhithe and New Cross! I took the last twenty steps two at a time, afraid now that a train would come and I would miss him. But there was no train. I caught my breath at the bottom of the staircase and then, keeping close to the wall, edged toward the platform. Carefully, I peered round.

Johnny Powers had vanished.

I continued down the platform. A bare brick ceiling curved over the station, open to the sky at the far end. The only sound was the drip of water from above. It was trick-ling through a confusion of plants and weeds that had some-how found some sort of life to cling onto against the old bricks. A rat scurried along between the rails and disappeared under the platform. There was no sign of Powers. But there was no other way out either. So he had to be here somewhere.

There was a drawing of the tunnel on the wall in front of me. The panel told me that it was the oldest tunnel in London, built by Marc Brunel between 1825 and 1842. In those days you'd have walked through or, I suppose, ridden in a horse-drawn carriage. Could you walk through now?

I went right up to the tunnel entrance and peered inside. There was no sound and somehow I didn't think Powers was inside. It was too dark, too dangerous. One false step, brush against the electric rail, and you'd fry. And there were the trains themselves, hurtling toward you through the darkness. You'd have to be crazy to walk down there. True, Johnny Powers was crazy. But the Fence surely wasn't—and neither was I.

I was about to leave when I noticed a door. A few steps led down from the platform at the very edge of the tunnel. There was a narrow walkway past three fire buckets and an antique fuse box. Then a brown door.

It seemed worth a try and there was no one around. I slid past the sign warning passengers not to proceed beyond this point and proceeded beyond it. At first I thought the door was locked. I pushed and I pulled without success. Just when I was about to give up, I realized that it was a sliding door. It slid open. I found a light switch and turned it on.

But the door was another disappointment. It opened into a small room, empty but for two telephones, a few scraps of litter, and about fifty years' worth of dust. One side led into a storage area. The other was covered by white tiles with a tap jutting out. If Powers had come in here, he wasn't here now. It led exactly nowhere. I turned the light off. Powers had lost me and I knew it. But I still didn't know how.

There was nothing for it but to go back to the house before I was missed. I took the elevator back to street level and hurried out of the station without being seen. Where had Powers gone? He hadn't taken a train and he couldn't have walked through the tunnel. There was nowhere to hide, no way could I have missed him. It seemed unfair. I'd thought he was going to lead me to the Fence. But it had just turned out to be a blind alley.

I kicked at an empty cigarette pack and walked back down the road with my hands in my pockets. If I hadn't been so disappointed I might have been a bit more alert. I remember that I heard the car coming but didn't think twice about it. When it slowed down, I should have reacted. I turned around when I heard its doors opening—but by then it was too late.

Somebody leaped on me from behind. I was pulled off my feet. I shouted out and tried to twist free. Then a fist hit me in the jaw. The strength drained out of me. Helpless, I was bundled into the car. And then we were away.

My mind was reeling. Half my teeth felt like they were about to say good-bye to the other half. I'd thought at first that I'd been caught by the police. But already I knew that it wasn't the police. No. This was something worse.

BIG ED

There were three of them in the car. I was in the backseat wedged between two of them. The third drove. There was a nodding dog on the ledge behind me. Only it wasn't nodding anymore because somebody had pulled off its head. That was the sort of people they were. The sort who could visit the Chamber of Horrors and upstage the exhibits.

The driver was a punk. He had close-cropped, bright green hair and two studs in his ear. There was a scorpion tattooed on the back of his neck. He was chewing gum and every time he moved his mouth the scorpion writhed like it was trying to find a way out of his skin. That was all I could see of him from where I was sitting. It was enough to make me wish that I was sitting someplace else.

The two other men—they were both in their thirties—could have been brothers. Or sisters. They were somewhere in between. The fat, unshaven cheeks, the enormous biceps, the beer guts, and the balding heads . . . that was all definitely masculine. I wasn't so sure about the handbags and the floral dresses. One of them had a scar running from his eye to his cheekbone. He'd tried to hide it with a dab of powder, but it needed something more. A large paper bag for example.

Nobody said anything for about five minutes, by which

time we'd crossed the river, heading southwest. I shifted in my seat and one of the heavies dug an elbow into my ribs.

"Keep still, pretty boy," he said in a voice so deep that it seemed to come from his knees.

"Where are we going?" I asked. "Who are you guys working for?"

"You'll find out soon enough."

The punk giggled, making the scorpion dance. I gritted my teeth. This wasn't the first time I'd been taken for a ride. But if I didn't make a move soon, it could well be the last. It didn't seem fair. I was too young to die. And to be murdered by two men in women's clothes! What would my parents say?

I made my move when the car slowed down for a red traffic light. I thought I'd timed it perfectly. We were in heavier traffic. One of the thugs was staring out of the window. The other was sitting back with his eyes half closed. Grab the handle, slam the door open, and I'd be out before they knew it. That was the idea.

But I'd underestimated them. I lurched forward. My hand moved a fraction. Then one of them grabbed me. I tried to shout out, to get the attention of the other drivers. I hadn't even opened my mouth before something hit me, hard, on the side of the neck. I think it was a handbag. The car spun. I thought of the nodding dog. Then I was out.

When I came to, I was back behind bars—but not exactly in a prison. It was a long narrow building that wasn't quite a building but was somehow familiar. My head was hurting and there was a nasty taste in my mouth. Otherwise I was more or less okay.

There was a sound outside. A rush and a shudder and a loud clinking. It told me what sort of building I was in. I should have known from the bare planks, the metal grille, the corridor almost as narrow as my prison cell, the square windows, and the communication cord. This was the guard's van of a train. But it was a train that wasn't moving. So where were we, then? Victoria Station?

I sat there for about two hours. It had been almost dark when I woke up, but now it was darker. I could see the light fading behind the screens that covered the windows. I expected the train to jolt forward at any time, but it never did. I was getting hungry. I hadn't eaten since breakfast and I was beginning to hope that a guard might wander through with a sandwich when the door opened and the punk appeared in the corridor.

He was still chewing gum and giggling. He had a safety pin in his nose and it wasn't just there for decoration. It was holding the whole thing together. He had the sort of face that looked like it could fall apart at any moment. Chalk white and rotten.

He produced a bundle of keys, unlocked the door, and slid it open. I got to my feet. "If you've come to check my ticket, I haven't got one," I said.

He giggled.

"Do you speak English?" I asked.

He jerked his head back the way he had come. He didn't speak at all.

I followed him out of the guard's van and across the coupling to the next carriage. The windows were uncovered here, and looking out, I saw that we were parked in a siding, next to some sort of stockyard. A tall stack of wood obstructed most of the view, but I could also see coils of barbed wire and oil drums. The yard was fenced off. There was nobody in sight.

We reached the second carriage. It was blocked off by a plain wooden door that looked out of place on a train. The punk knocked and opened it. We went in.

Classical music. That was the first thing I heard. Bach or Vivaldi played on an expensive stereo system. The whole carriage had been revamped by an interior designer with expensive tastes. Silk wallpaper, silk curtains, two more chandeliers . . . the furniture could have come straight out of Woburn Abbey. A cocktail cabinet stood beside the door. One of the walls was lined with books. There was a fireplace at the far end with one of those artificial fires blazing artificially.

The two charm sisters from the car were sitting together on a chaise longue. One of them was reading a romance novel. The other was knitting. There were two other people in the room. One was a woman, wearing a satin dress that was tight in all the right places and tighter still in some of the wrong ones. Her hair was the sort of vivid blond that can only come out of a bottle. The other was a man. I guessed he was in charge.

He was around fifty, wearing a dressing gown with wide lapels and a cravat. He had a shock of white hair, so white that it did look as if he'd had a shock. His eyes were almost colorless, too. He was smoking a cigarette in a long black holder and sipping a martini.

"Good evening," he said. "I'm Big Ed."

I shrugged. "You don't look that big to me," I said.

One of the sisters looked up from his book. He was the one who'd hit me. "You don't talk to Big Ed like that," he grunted.

"Why not?" I asked. I rubbed the back of my neck. "He gave me a big 'eadache."

The punk giggled again. Big Ed flicked ash from his cigarette.

"Nicholas Diamond," he said. He had a soft, tired voice that was almost a whisper. "It's very nice to see you. I have to say that I was dying to meet you."

"Shame you couldn't do it sooner," I said.

He ignored me. "I had my boys out looking for Johnny Powers," he went on. "It was his good luck that they missed him. And your bad luck that they found you." He put down the cigarette and swirled the olive in his glass. "We'll catch up with him later. But the question now is, what do we do with his number two?"

"How about a drink and a sandwich?" I suggested.

He shook his head. "Oh no. You see, I had a gun sent in to Strangeday Hall. Three of my boys were going to rub Johnny Powers. It seems you got in the way. One of them was burned—Blondie's his name. Now his own mother doesn't recognize him. And the thing is, you see, she's my sister. Blondie is my nephew."

That was bad news. Uncle Ed wasn't smiling anymore and there was a flicker of color in his eyes—a dull red.

"I'd like to know where Powers is," he said. "I could ask you. But of course you wouldn't say."

"I don't know," I muttered. "We could come to some sort of arrangement . . ."

"I don't think so." His lips curled. "The only arrangements you should be thinking of are the ones for your funeral."

He stood up. I thought of attacking him, maybe grabbing an antique lamp and going for his head, but I quickly forgot it. The punk was right behind me. And the two charm sisters had already shown how fast they could move.

"I'm going to get Johnny Powers," Big Ed continued. "South London and East London will be mine. What's the world coming to when you've got kids running the rackets? I don't like kids. I don't like you, Diamond. That's why you've got to go."

He waved a hand and I was gone.

The punk was the first to move, lunging forward to grab me from behind. "Take him out and do it, Spike," he ordered. "Scarface and Tootsie—you go with him." The two drag artists stood up. "Good-bye, Diamond," he said. "Remember Blondie. Remember me. And have a nice death."

I was dragged out of the carriage. It must have been double glazed because as soon as I was out in the night air I could hear the trains, clanking and rattling through the darkness. It had begun to rain. At first it was a light drizzle, but as I was pulled, kicking and fighting, through the stockyard and onto the rails, it came down more heavily. It was a real cloudburst. In seconds the four of us were drenched.

Because of the rain I saw little of my surroundings. I could just make out the lights of a station—it was Clapham Junction—blinking in the distance.

We crossed about six or seven rails, our feet crunching on the gravel. Once we stopped as an Intercity Express thundered past, the windows a blur of yellow. I thought someone might see us, but in the darkness and the swirling rain that was impossible. Then the punk pushed me between the shoulders. I stumbled and fell. Tootsie and Scarface seized my arms and legs, and before I knew what was happening, they were tying me down across the rails. The practiced way they worked made me think that they must have done it before. It took them less than a minute. But when they straightened up I was fixed as firmly as an oven-ready chicken. My hands were tied to one rail, my legs to the other.

My neck rested on the cold metal. My body slumped in between.

Then Tootsie squatted down beside me. His hair was all

over his face and his makeup was running. But he was smiling.

"Only one more train runs on this track tonight," he said. "It comes in about ten minutes. It doesn't stop until it gets to Waterloo Station. It won't stop for you."

"Wait . . ." I began, but then he stuffed a handkerchief into my mouth. I tried to spit it out. He twisted another loop of rope around my head, gagging me.

"No one will see you," he hissed. "No one will hear you. Ten minutes. Think about it, pretty boy. In ten minutes you won't be so pretty no more."

The punk giggled one last time. Tootsie stood up and adjusted his dress. Then, linking arms with Scarface, he walked away. I was left alone, spread out on the track. The rain was falling harder than ever.

OFF THE RAILS

One day I'm going to write a book. It will be called *Sticky Situations* by N. Diamond. But don't look for a chapter called "How to Untie Yourself from Rails in the Pouring Rain with an Intercity 125 Thundering Toward You at 90 mph." You won't find it. Because I tell you now, it can't be done.

As soon as Tootsie, Spike, and Scarface had gone, I tried to move my feet, but I could barely wiggle my toes. I tried to slide my hands under the rope. I had about as much chance of flying. They had tied me down tight. The rope was biting into my flesh, cutting off the circulation. The rain didn't help either. It was coming down so hard that it was blinding me, making it impossible to see what I was doing. But I suppose that it didn't matter too much. I was doing precisely nothing. There was nothing I could do.

There was a sudden rumble in the air. I wriggled around just in time to see an enormous train come battering through the rain. At least it looked enormous from where I was lying. I tried to call out but the gag stopped me. Now I could see the driver, smoking, high up in the front of the train. My whole body stiffened, waiting for it to ride over me. I think I muttered a prayer.

The train was almost on top of me. Then there was a loud

clattering sound and it jerked away to one side. Someone, somewhere had changed the switches.

The rain sliced down. Somewhere a light blinked from red to green. I heard a click as another switch was changed and a rail slid across to carry the next train to its correct destination. A solitary pigeon flew in a ragged arc above me. The clouds rolled over.

Suddenly I was trembling. That was strange because I thought I'd been trembling all along. But then I realized that it wasn't just me. It was the rails beneath me. They were vibrating, softly at first but more violently with every second that passed. I couldn't hear anything. I couldn't see anything. But I knew the train was approaching. And this time it was approaching on my track.

I think I went berserk right then. I struggled furiously, my body heaving, my arms and legs tearing at the ropes. But it was useless. All I managed to do was to bruise my ankles and tear my trousers. I forced myself to go limp. Things weren't so bad, I told myself. I mean, there are worse things in life than being run over by a train. I tried to think of one of them. I couldn't. I went berserk again.

I was still heaving and twisting when I heard the blast of the whistle in the distance. It scoured through the night like a red-hot poker. The train couldn't have been more than a mile away. That gave me perhaps a couple of minutes of life. Here lies Nick Diamond, aged thirteen years, seven months, and a couple of minutes. Rest in pieces.

Then the man appeared.

I think it was a man. He had come out of nowhere. He was standing over me, his head about a mile away from his feet. He was wearing a parka with the hood drawn over his head and in the slanting rain I couldn't make out his face.

"Ngg," I said. "Mmn, ngg, nyun . . ." It wasn't easy making polite conversation with the gag.

The man leaned down and suddenly I saw there was a knife in his hand. Before I could react he reached out and cut through the ropes holding my wrists. I sat up, tearing at the gag. The rails were shaking like crazy now. It felt like a long electric shock.

The man dropped the knife and walked away. He hadn't said a word. I had no idea who he was—and yet somewhere in the back of my mind I thought I knew him. Thickset, wide shoulders. Perhaps a wisp of fair hair showing under the hood. That was all I saw. He had already gone.

"Come back!" I shouted.

He ignored me and I didn't shout again. The last thing I wanted to do was to let Big Ed know I was free, and anyway there was no time for a chat. I could see the train now. The window at the front glowed like a Cyclops' eye. I snatched up the knife and hacked at the ropes holding my ankles. My arms wouldn't obey me. The knife slipped out and I winced as I managed to stab myself in the foot. The train was only yards away now. The bellow of the engine filled my ears. I cut one rope—then the other. The train crashed forward. But I was free. I threw myself off the rails. Another second and it would have been too late.

Ker-thud, ker-thud, ker-thud, ker-thud . . .

It might have been the wheels of the train. It might have been the sound of my own heart. But that was all I heard as I lay there, clutching the ground. The train went past, traveling between me and my mysterious rescuer. By the time it had gone, he had vanished.

I stood up and staggered to keep my balance. I'd torn my trousers, gashed my leg. I was soaking wet and bruised all over. But I had to admit, I'd have been in worse shape if I hadn't been cut free. Who had it been? And how had he found me?

I didn't intend to stand around in the middle of Clapham Junction working out the answers. That could come later. Right now I had to get away—but even as I moved I realized that my problems were far from over. If I went back to Wapping, I'd have to explain my absence to Johnny and his mother. Worse still, Tim had been alone with them for the best part of twelve hours. Twelve hours with him and they'd be sure to smell a rat—a dirty rat, it went without saying.

Somehow I had to win back their trust. And the best way to do that was sitting only a hundred yards away in a disused railway siding. I had a score to settle with Big Ed anyway. I was cold, bruised, soaked, and exhausted. And I was angry. There was nothing Johnny wouldn't do for me if I took Big Ed out of the picture.

I even had an idea how to go about it. I went back to the siding. The oil drums. I'd noticed them when they'd taken me out to the rails . . . ten barrels with two words stenciled in red on each of them. HIGHLY FLAMMABLE. Just then the same two words applied to my temper. These weren't nice people. It was high time something horrible happened to them.

There were no lights on behind the windows as I approached Big Ed's carriage. I was afraid he might have posted guards, but there was nobody around. The rain was beginning to slacken off. Fortunately the moon was still hidden behind thick cloud. Careful not to make a sound, I limped away from the carriage and over to the oil drums. I tapped one with a finger. It was full. Each drum was secured with a metal cap set in the top near the rim. I tried turning one. At first it resisted and I thought it had rusted firm. But by using the knife, cutting into the groove, I was able to free it. I opened four of the cans. The rich, chemical smell filled my nostrils.

I rolled the first of the drums across the yard until it came to rest against the wheels of the front carriage—the one with the chandeliers and cocktail cabinet. The oil or whatever it was slopped out, forming a sticky pool on the ground. I was careful not to get any of it on me, but by the time I'd finished I still smelled like a garage on a busy day. I rolled three of the cans across, one for each carriage. Apart from the crunch of gravel and the gurgle of escaping oil, I made no sound. Five minutes later, a miniature lake had formed around Ed's hideout. And still the oil spluttered out of the open drums.

Wiping my hands on my trousers—it made them dirtier rather than cleaner—I went back to the fourth can. This one I rolled in the opposite direction, away from the carriages and back onto the rails. Hoisting it up onto the rails themselves was the difficult part. It weighed a ton. But after that it was easy. The rims fitted neatly onto the rails and with no friction it rolled effortlessly. There was a slight gradient down to Clapham Junction Station and I had no trouble with the switches. Using only one hand I was able to roll it all the way, leaving a trail of glimmering oil behind me.

By now you should have gotten the picture: a pool of highly flammable liquid underneath Big Ed's hideout; a long trail of the same stuff leading down to the station. *Light the blue wick and retire quickly,* as it says on your average firework. I had fireworks in mind—and Big Ed was about to put in for permanent retirement.

Clapham Junction Station had shut down for the night by the time I got there. Now what I needed was a match. It took me a while but in the end I was lucky. Someone had left a pack in the waiting room with one match inside.

I found a phone booth and dialed 0. The operator came on and asked me which service I wanted. I told her police. There was a click, a pause, then a voice. "This is the police. What number are you calling from?"

"Listen," I said. "Are you interested in finding Big Ed?"

My words were met by a long silence. I could imagine the confusion at the other end. There was another click. Perhaps they were trying to trace the call. That didn't bother me. I'd be gone long before they arrived.

"Hello, caller?" another voice asked. Or maybe it was the same voice. I didn't care.

"I know where you can find Big Ed," I said. "If you want him."

"Who is this speaking?"

"Never mind that." I shivered. It had gotten colder. "Do you want him or don't you?"

"We want him." This was the second voice. They must have transferred the call even as I was speaking. "Where is he?"

"He has two railway carriages in a siding just outside Clapham Junction Station," I said. "Next to the stockyard."

"There are lots of stockyards around there," the voice said. "How do we know which one is his?"

I didn't answer. Propping the telephone under my chin, I struck the match. It glared up in the confined space of the phone booth. With the fumes of the oil all around me, I was surprised we didn't blow up then and there. I threw the match onto the platform. The oil caught fire.

I watched the flames scurry across the platform, over the edge, and onto the rails. Like some sort of mythical animal, with feathers of fire, it sped into the night, heading for Big Ed's carriage.

"How do we find him, caller?" the voice insisted.

"It won't be difficult," I said. And hung up.

WORLD'S END

I was more careful when I left Clapham Junction. I was still soaking wet. I stank of oil. I had to cross London with just about the entire population on the lookout for me. And when I got back to Wapping, I'd probably be shot. But otherwise I didn't have anything to worry about. I was having a really lovely day.

I stepped into the shadows as a couple of police cars raced past, sirens screaming. Perhaps it was seeing them that made up my mind for me. There was no point in going back to Johnny Powers and his gang quite yet. Even if they did lead me to the Fence, there would be little I could do with the information. Because with Snape and Boyle dead, who would believe my story?

But just suppose somebody had seen the two policemen when they visited me at the school? Chief Inspector Snape and his unsmiling assistant weren't the sort of people you could forget in a hurry. If I could prove that they'd been there before the Woburn Abbey incident, the rest of my story might be more credible. The only question was—who might have seen them? It had been late on a Tuesday afternoon when they had come. Everyone else had gone home. That's what they had been waiting for—to catch me there alone.

But there was one person: Peregrine Palis would have been there. It would have been just like him to stay behind in the staff room to make sure I didn't slip away. And the staff room was directly between the front entrance and my class-room. If anyone had seen the two policemen, it would have been him. And I knew where the French teacher lived. He had a flat just off the King's Road near the bit known as World's End. I could go there now. It was less far to walk than Wap-ping. And I'd almost certainly find him in.

I set off, keeping to the shadows. There were a surpris-ing number of cars about, considering how late it was. Each time one passed me I shivered and tried to hide my face. If a police car had chosen that moment to cross the bridge, you could have kissed good-bye to the next chapter.

In fact, I made it as far as Chelsea before I was spotted. I'd reached the traffic lights on the King's Road and stopped to get my bearings. There were two policemen standing on the other side of the road, outside a bank. At first they didn't let on they'd seen me. After all, as far as they knew I was armed and dangerous. Out of the corner of my eye I saw one nudge the other and then talk into the edge of his jacket. He wasn't having a conversation with his armpit. There would be a radio there. He was calling for help.

Casually, I turned left and began to walk down the King's Road to World's End. I didn't need to look back to know that the two policemen were following me. But I still kept up the pretense. I was just an ordinary, innocent boy out for a night walk. The rags and the smell of oil? Nothing to concern you, Officer. I always dress this way. I turned a corner and for a moment I was out of their sight. I began to run.

It was already too late. I'd seen it the moment I'd set off—a police car, heading toward me at seventy miles an hour. And it had seen me, too.

Suddenly the sirens and blue lights were on and it was swerving across the road to cut me off. With a spurt of energy, I took a sharp left, past a pub and down a narrow street. I heard the screech of wheels as the police car followed me. There was a Dumpster parked outside a development of new flats. I didn't look to see what was inside it. I just dived in headfirst.

The police car tore around the corner and continued down the road. I knew I had perhaps half a minute before it turned around and came back. I climbed out of the Dumpster and realized where I was. The building behind me was where Palis lived. It was an apartment house, a smart place with smoked-glass windows, private balconies, and sophisticated burglar alarms. But then of course this was Chelsea, where you'd expect sophisticated burglars. I'd often wondered how a French teacher at an ordinary school could afford such a posh address. But this was no time to ask questions.

I pulled myself up onto the low wall that surrounded the building and from there I was able to climb onto the slanting roof of what must have been a boiler room. But that was as far as I got. A headlight swept through the darkness and I knew that the police car had returned. This time it stopped right beneath me. There was a click as the door opened and two men got out.

"Any sign of him?" one asked.

"No. He must have doubled back."

"You sure it was him?"

"No doubt about it. A right little villain . . ."

Well, I wasn't going to argue with that, provided they went away and left me alone. But then the worst thing possible happened. A light went on overhead. It slanted down, capturing me in a bright square. A door opened and somebody strutted out, leaning over the balcony to call down to the policemen.

"What's going on?" a voice demanded. It was a voice that I knew well.

I looked up. Palis had come out onto the balcony, wearing a blue dressing gown and pajamas. He was leaning over, looking down at the policemen. From where he was standing, I was directly in his line of vision. He saw me. He couldn't miss me. For a moment he frowned and I froze. One word from him and it would all be over. Desperately I raised a finger to my lips and stared at him with pleading eyes.

"We're looking for someone," one of the policemen said. "A young boy."

"Well, do you have to make such an infernal racket about it?" Palis asked, and I breathed again. For the moment I was safe.

"He's dangerous, sir," the policeman said.

"And so am I when I'm woken up in the middle of the night," Palis snapped. "He obviously isn't here, so I suggest you go and wake up somebody else looking for him."

There was a bit more muffled chat below, but then the police car moved away and the two policemen passed underneath the building and back into the King's Road. Palis glanced at me. "Nicholas Simple?" he demanded in a tone of disbelief.

"Yes, sir." I stood up. "Thank you very much, Mr. Palis—sir."

"You'd better climb up here before anyone sees you," he said.

I climbed over the rail and joined him on the terrace. "Thank you," I said. "For not turning me in . . ."

He smiled. "Well, I had a good reason . . ."

"I'm innocent," I blurted out. "I didn't do any of it. In fact, I was working for the police from the very start. I still am. Only . . . it's difficult to explain."

"You'd better come in," he said.

I followed him into the flat.

I found myself in a comfortable room with copies of paintings by Rubens and Picasso on the walls. The carpet was so thick my foot almost disappeared when I walked and the lighting was low and soft. I'd expected to see some sign of school—French books or homework or something—but there was nothing. Maybe he kept his work in another room.

"Sit down," Palis said. "I'll make you some tea."

"Thank you, Mr. Palis." I sat down beside the table. "And thanks again for not telling the police. Why didn't you?" I remembered what he'd said out on the terrace. "You said there was a reason . . ."

"Exactement." Palis nodded. "I never believed that you were really responsible for the theft of the carbuncle, Nicholas. Your French is poor. You are often inattentive. But despite all the evidence, I found it hard to believe that you could have allowed yourself to commit such a terrible crime.

"So tell me your story," he said. "You say you're working for the police . . ."

"Yes, sir—Mr. Palis," I replied. "That's why I came to see you. Do you remember the time you made me write out all the tenses of *rire* when I was mucking around in class?"

"Yes." He frowned. "I don't think you've handed them in yet."

"I'll do them tonight, sir."

"No, no. They can wait. Go on . . ."

"Well, that was when they came. I wondered if you saw them. It was a Tuesday afternoon. Two men . . . Snape and Boyle. Big and ugly."

He shook his head. "I left the school early that day," he said. "I went to the library with *The Hunchback of Notre Dame.*"

"Could he have seen them?"

"I mean the book."

"Oh."

So that was that. Palis hadn't seen anything. But once I'd started I had to go on. In answer to his questions I told him everything that had happened to me since then. He didn't interrupt. I couldn't tell whether he believed me or not. By the time I finished, my tea was stone-cold. I hadn't had a chance to drink it.

"This Penelope . . ." he muttered. "You were sent to find her?"

"Yes."

"Well, if you can do that maybe your troubles will be over."

"If anyone believes me," I said gloomily.

He straightened up. "I believe you," he said. "I don't know why. It is *un vrai conte.*"

"An old count?" I translated.

"No. An extraordinary story. But I do believe you. The question is—what can I do to help you?"

There was no real answer to that. If Palis hadn't seen Snape, then coming here tonight had been a complete waste of time.

"I'll go," I said.

"In the morning." He got to his feet. "Right now you need a hot bath and somewhere to sleep. I have a spare room. Tomorrow I can drive you to Wapping. It seems to me that the sooner you rejoin your brother and this . . . Powers, the better."

"It may be too late already."

"Do you have any choice, *mon ami?*"

I spent the rest of the night in a spare room the size of a cupboard. It was almost like being back in my cell except that the door wasn't locked. I fell asleep clutching the pillow. And I dreamed. I dreamed of Tim in his gangster outfit. I dreamed of Johnny Powers and a lion and an Intercity 125 Express. I thought I heard the tinkle of a bell and somebody talking in a low voice, but then the voice became that of the judge sentencing me and I found myself strapped down and realized that I was in the electric chair with Ma Powers about to throw the switch. I saw her hand move. There was a flash of light and I opened my eyes.

The sun was shining through the window, dazzling me. I was awake. And I'd managed to tear the pillow in half.

DOORWAY TO HELL

I'd been wrong about Peregrine Palis. Okay, he had a stupid name. He was short and fat. And he taught French. But nobody's perfect and I had to admit—as he drove me back to Wapping the next day—that he couldn't have been more helpful. Anyone else would have called the police and turned me in. But not only did he take me back, he even bought me a new jacket and shirt from the local market. He said I could pay him back when I managed to prove my innocence.

It was Sunday and Wapping was even emptier than the day before. The rain hadn't left it any prettier either. With no gutters, the roads had nowhere to put the water. It was lying there in wide pools, dirty mirrors reflecting a dirty sky. Mr. Palis stopped near the subway station and I got out.

"Thanks, Mr. Palis . . ." I began.

"Good luck," he said. He was in a hurry to get away. "I hope it all works out. If you need help, get in touch."

"I will."

He drove off. His back wheel smashed one of the mirrors, spraying my nice new clothes with mud and water. I took a deep breath. There was nobody around. Now all I had to do was to face up to Johnny Powers and persuade him that I was still on his side.

The real worry was Tim. He'd been alone with Powers for almost twenty-four hours. I'd have been worried if it had been twenty-four minutes. They'd have asked him questions. Would he have come up with the right answers? One word out of place and he could reserve a place in the nearest cemetery. But Mr. Palis had been right. I had no choice. If I didn't go back, Tim wouldn't stand a chance.

I walked down Wapping High Street to the turnoff where the hideout stood—or rather leaned against its scaffolding. It all seemed quiet enough. Even so I was aware of a sort of tingling. Call it an alarm bell, if you like. Something was wrong but I didn't know what it was. Maybe it was too quiet. Maybe it was something else. Something I'd seen or heard.

I stopped beside the front door. I lifted my finger to ring the bell, then thought better of it. Powers wasn't expecting visitors. It would be just like him to put a dozen bullets through the door before he opened it. I went back to the window and peered through. The curtains were drawn. Were they still in bed?

I reached out again for the bell. And that was when I saw it.

It was the color that saved me. Wapping was all gray—with the occasional patches of dark brown and black. After a while, your eyes get used to it. You didn't expect to see any color. But this was bright yellow. It was a piece of plastic, about an inch long. It was lying on the doorstep. I knelt down and picked it up. There were a couple of copper strands inside. It was a piece of electrical wiring. What was it doing there?

I looked back at the doorbell and suddenly I didn't like it at all. Because suddenly I remembered that when we'd arrived at the hideout there hadn't been a doorbell. It was brand-new. It had been put there specially for me.

Right then I wanted to turn around and go back to the subway station. I could go to the very end of the East London Line and sit there quietly until it was all over. But there was still a chance that Tim was inside. I made up my mind.

I followed the houses around to the back and went in the way I'd come out—up the pile of rubble and in through my bedroom window. It was harder going up than it had been jumping down. I could only just reach the windowsill, and when I finally managed to pull myself up, the window was locked. I used my elbow to break the glass. If Johnny and his mother were asleep, I'd wake them up for sure. But I didn't think they were there. I didn't think they'd been there for quite some time.

A little piece of yellow wire . . .

I hurried through the bedroom, noticing that Tim's bed had been slept in. Nothing else seemed to have been disturbed. Nobody stirred as I moved out into the corridor, but walking down the stairs, I heard a sort of muffled crying. I reached the bottom and stopped dead. I think about two minutes passed before I even dared to move.

Tim was sitting in a chair, tied up and gagged. He was still

dressed in a pair of pajamas—but perhaps as a joke, someone had put the gangster hat back on his head. He was staring at an object on a table only a couple of yards away from
him. It was a Walt Disney alarm clock with Mickey Mouse
pointing at the time with his white-gloved hands: seven minutes to eleven. But I didn't think Walt Disney had been responsible for the rest of it. There were six sticks of dynamite
attached to the clock. A yellow wire trailed away, leading to
the door.

A time bomb. It was set for eleven o'clock. Ring the doorbell and it would have gone off sooner. Tim, myself, and
Mickey Mouse would have been blown to smithereens.

I forced myself to move. Tim had seen me out of the corner of his eye and he was rocking back and forth and grunt-
ing. I took the gag off.

"Hello, Tim," I said.

"Nick!" he screamed. "Get me out of here! Help! Do
something! Call the police! Call the bomb squad! Where have
you been? How could you do this to me?"

For a moment I was tempted to gag him again. I had to
move quickly and having him yelling at me wouldn't help.
There was no time to untie him. Powers had used wire and it
wouldn't cut. The clock showed six minutes to eleven. In six
minutes I might just manage to free his legs, but Tim was
such a gibbering wreck that I doubted he'd be able to use
them.

"This is all your fault," he went on. "I should never have

helped you escape. It's not fair. What did I ever do to hurt anyone? I should have listened to Mum . . ."

I went over to the table and examined the bomb. It was more complicated than I'd first thought. Apart from the yellow wire there were two coils—red and blue—leading from the dynamite to the clock via a sort of black plastic junction box. The box was closed by a single screw. There was a glass cylinder next to it, a bit like a valve. The whole thing was tied together by two strips of plastic tape.

"What are you going to do?" Tim whined.

"I'm going to defuse it," I said.

"But where is the fuse?" Tim whimpered.

"I don't know."

He fell silent again.

I reached out and touched the dynamite. My hand was trembling so hard that my fingers were just a blur. It didn't go off. Five minutes to eleven. I tried to think what I knew about bomb disposal. Unfortunately it wasn't one of the subjects they taught at school. But I'd seen films and read books. At eleven o'clock the alarm bell would ring. An electrical contact would be made. The detonator—that was presumably the glass valve—would be activated. It would be the last thing I would see.

Ringing the doorbell would have done the same thing, only earlier. How else could I set the bomb off? It could have a touch sensor of some sort, but I'd already touched it and it hadn't sensed anything. I could cut one of the wires. But I didn't know which one and anyway it was too dangerous. I could move the hands of the clock back. That seemed the most obvious thing to do. In fact it was so obvious that it was probably lethal.

My eyes were drawn to the junction box with its single screw. That had to be the answer. Break the electrical circuit and the whole thing would be neutralized. I'd left my knife at World's End. I needed a screwdriver or something with a narrow blade. I straightened up.

"Where are you going?" Tim demanded.

"To the kitchen," I said.

"The kitchen?" Tim jerked around. "Nick—this is no time for a cup of tea!"

I ignored him. A minute later I was back with a vegetable knife. It wasn't perfect but at least the blade was flat at the top. Another minute. There were only four left.

My hand was still shaking. I paused for a few seconds and fought to control myself.

Three minutes to eleven.

I leaned down and inserted the tip of the knife into the hole at the top of the black box. It slipped and the blade brushed against one of the wires. My heart did a double backward somersault and dived into my stomach. I was sweating now. I could feel it trickling down the sides of my face. Using all my concentration, I pushed the knife back into the right place. It came into contact with the screw. I turned it.

The screw wouldn't move. I tried again, harder. This time

I felt the screw give. But would there be another fail-safe device? Would turning the screw be enough to set the whole thing off? It was too late to stop. The knife made three complete revolutions. The screw rose up then fell out. It landed on the table with a little rattle. Tim squeaked.

I put the knife down and reached for the lid of the box with my finger and thumb. They had never felt bigger or more clumsy. I didn't know how much time had passed. I didn't dare to look at the clock. Somehow I got a grip on the plastic and pulled as gently as I could, looking for a wire or a spring mechanism that might join it together. There was nothing. I dropped the lid and wiped the sweat out of my eyes. So far so good.

I had been right about the electrical circuit. Inside the junction box there was a wire and an ordinary switch. It had three positions. At the moment it was in the middle. I could push it to either side. But which side? Make the wrong choice and I wouldn't be given another. I glanced at the clock. I had less than a minute to decide.

"Left or right, Tim?" I called out.

"Left or right what?" he asked.

"Just say—left or right."

"Left."

"Left?"

"Right."

"Right?"

"No, I mean . . . left's got to be right. Left!"

I pushed the switch to the right. The alarm bell rang. Tim screamed. But the clock just went on ticking. Mickey Mouse grinned at me. I felt all the strength drain out of me. I'd done it.

It took me half an hour to untie Tim. My hands were still shaking at the end of it. At last he stood up, took one last look at the bomb, and went off to get dressed.

I sank limply into his chair. I'd done it. I still couldn't believe it. Upstairs I could hear Tim thumping about in the bedroom. I sighed. He could at least have remembered to say thanks.

PENELOPE

Ma Powers had left a bit of food in the kitchen and Tim cooked lunch. He burned the toast and his eggs weren't so much scrambled as cemented, but I was hungry enough to eat anything. It's funny how extreme danger can give you a big appetite. I'd had two close calls in less than twenty-four hours and it seemed like my stomach was celebrating. I'd drunk three cups of coffee and eaten half a pack of biscuits before I knew what I was doing. If I stayed in this game much longer I was going to get fat. Or dead.

I told Tim what had happened since I'd left my encounter with Big Ed and my night with Mr. Palis. We thought of phoning the teacher again but there didn't seem much point.

"So who was it, then?" Tim asked.

"Who?"

"The person who cut you free from the railway."

I shrugged. "I've no idea. At least, I thought I'd seen him somewhere before but . . . in the rain, it was impossible to tell." I cast my mind back to the night before. "I don't even know how he found me—if it was a he. I was in the middle of nowhere. Nobody knew I was there. It doesn't make sense . . ."

There was less to puzzle about in Tim's side of the story. In fact, I could more or less guess what had happened to him without asking. Left alone with Johnny Powers and with me mysteriously gone, he would have been lucky if he'd lasted ten minutes.

And that was about it. Johnny had gotten back from wherever he'd been to find me missing. He'd questioned Tim and he hadn't liked the answers. Suspicion is a fast-growing seed and with Tim around it had had plenty of fertilizer. He hadn't been invited to the big gangster meeting in the afternoon. The atmosphere during dinner had been as frozen as the fishsticks Nails Nathan had served. Tim had gone to bed early only to be dragged out at dawn. Johnny had decided not to take any chances. Tim had been tied up and gagged . . . and the rest I knew.

"Did he say anything?" I asked.

"He didn't say anything nice," Tim muttered.

"I'm sure." I sighed. "But did he say anything that might tell us where he is now?"

Tim thought for a moment. "He told a sort of joke just as he left," he said. "That guy Needles Nathan had fixed up the bomb and he said it would blow us both sky-high. Then Powers said that was okay because by the time you got back, they'd have gone underground."

"Underground? Was there anything else?"

"Yes. That was when he put the hat on me. He said

something about going to the bank. But he hoped that when the bomb went off, they'd be able to hear it."

Tim had told me what I wanted to know. If Powers hoped to hear the explosion, that had to mean he was somewhere near. "Going underground" could mean he was simply hiding or it could mean something more. As for the bank, that didn't make any sense at all. For one thing, there were no banks in the area and anyway this was Sunday. They would all be closed.

I hadn't said anything, but Tim must have read my thoughts because he suddenly bolted upright in his chair.

"You're not going to look for him, are you?" he groaned.

"What other choice do we have?" I asked.

"How about going home and forgetting all about it?"

"The police are still looking for us," I reminded him.

"For you," Tim said.

"For us. You helped me escape, remember?"

And so we left. Tim had changed into more ordinary clothes and I was still wearing the gear that Mr. Palis had given me. As always, there was nobody around in Wapping, but if anyone happened to pass, they probably wouldn't give us a second glance. I'd found a small backpack in the cupboard upstairs and I took that, too—to make me look more ordinary, I told Tim.

But that wasn't quite true. I'd defused the bomb, and while the switch in the junction box remained on the right, I was fairly sure that it was harmless. So I took it with me in the backpack. Who could say? It might come in handy.

We spent the rest of the day going around in circles. The light was failing before I realized that we were, too. We hadn't found anything. There were a hundred and one places Powers could have chosen to hide out in . . . empty apartment buildings, construction sites, half-built houses, and even derelict mobile homes.

"If only Snape hadn't gotten killed," I muttered.

We'd paused for breath, sitting on a low wall beside Wapping High Street. My prison shoes were still pinching and I'd walked enough for one day.

"I thought you didn't like him," Tim said.

"I didn't. But right now he's the one person we could go to. He knew the truth. He might be able to help us."

We didn't speak for a while. Then Tim frowned. "Are you sure there aren't any banks around here?" he asked.

"Banks?"

"I'm sure that's what Powers said. He was going to the bank."

"But the banks are closed."

"So? He could still rob one."

Banks. Banks . . .

Suddenly it hit me. I felt so stupid I could have hit myself. We were sitting only half a minute away from the biggest bank in London and I hadn't even thought of it. I got to my feet and threw my backpack across my shoulders, forgetting for a moment what was inside. It would have been just my luck to blow myself to pieces just as I was getting somewhere.

"Where are we going?" Tim asked.

"To the bank," I said.

I retraced the steps we'd taken the morning we'd arrived, back between two warehouses and out onto the jetty. I stopped at the end and looked around. As I remembered, it gave me a good view of the edge of Wapping. Tim caught up with me and stopped, scratching his head. "What are you doing?" he demanded.

"The bank, Tim," I said. I pointed. "The riverbank. That's what Powers was talking about. He's got to be somewhere here. Right now we're probably looking at him."

But what were we looking at? First there were the warehouses—King Henry's Wharf on the one side, St. John's on the other. Cranes perched on the vertical walls like gigantic grasshoppers, feeding on the brickwork. Farther away were the new apartments and more jetties with the silver-gray water lapping at their legs. And there was the abandoned houseboat, moored to the dock. There was still something strange about it. I'd noticed it the first time I'd seen it, but now I couldn't remember what it was. I looked more closely. There was something wrong, but suddenly it didn't matter anymore.

The sun was low and it was hard to see, but I could still make out the single word painted on the side of the boat. I might have seen it before if I'd been looking for it. Like all houseboats it had a name. And the name was *Penelope.*

"That's it!" I said. "Penelope!"

Tim had seen it, too. "So when Powers said he was going to Penelope . . ." he began.

"He was talking about the houseboat. That must have been where his meeting with the Fence was."

"But you said he went into the station."

"He did." I thought back. "He must have realized he was being followed. So he used the station to lose me."

"So what do we do now?" Tim asked.

"Now? We have a closer look at that boat."

But that was easier said than done. We followed the road around again only to find that the dock was blocked off by a tall gate with barbed wire at the top. There was no way we could climb over it and no way around the side. That only left one alternative. Fortunately the day had been warm.

"You've got to be joking!" Tim exclaimed when I told him.

"You don't have to come," I muttered, unbuttoning my shirt.

"There's got to be another way . . ."

"Can you think of one?"

Tim thought. Then he unbuckled his belt.

"You're coming with me?" I asked.

"Somebody's got to look after you," he said.

We left our clothes and the backpack at the end of the jetty and, wearing only underpants, slipped into the river. It had been a warm day, only the Thames hadn't noticed. The water was freezing. By the time I'd gotten in as far as my knees, I couldn't feel my toes.

The current was strong and it was moving against us. Tim followed me, doing a dog paddle that would have disgraced a dog. As well as being around zero degrees, the water was also filthy. A lot of nasty things floated past on a level with my nose. I tried to swim faster, but every three strokes I took I was pulled back two. Fortunately it wasn't too far to the boat. But it was still a good five minutes before I hauled myself out.

And that wasn't easy either. The deck of the *Penelope* was a long way above the water, and although I pulled on the side of the boat, it refused to tilt. In the end, Tim had to help me up, pushing from underneath and disappearing under the surface himself at the same time. Then I was lying on the deck, reaching out for him while he coughed and spluttered with a dead fish caught behind his ear. Somehow I pulled him out.

I don't quite know what I was expecting to find on board. I certainly wasn't going to catch Johnny Powers there. In fact, the only thing I was likely to catch was pneumonia. And once we'd gotten inside, it looked as if the whole thing had just been a big waste of time.

The boat was empty. There was one big cabin contained in a sort of wooden box with narrow windows and a wide doorway leading onto the deck. The wheel and the engine controls would have been mounted outside, but they were long gone. The *Penelope* was a rusting hulk, nothing more. A single room about the size of a bus, floating on the Thames with nowhere to go.

Tim was standing in the corner, shivering. The fish, hanging beside his face, stared at him.

"Why do I ever listen to you?" he began, stammering on every word as his teeth beat out a flamenco rhythm.

"Wait a minute . . ." I cut in.

It wasn't much to go on. It certainly wasn't worth the swim. But now I reached down and picked it up. It was a piece of black-and-white paper, crumpled into a ball.

"What is it?" Tim asked.

"It's a piece of black-and-white paper, crumpled into a ball," I said. I opened it up and read a single word—*Licorice*. As chewed by Johnny Powers. "He was here," I said.

"Well, he isn't here now."

"No. But maybe he'll come back."

"Nick . . ."

"All right," I said. "Let's move."

Together we made our way back onto the deck. I was still vaguely aware that there was something wrong. The *Penelope* wasn't behaving like a boat should. I didn't know what it was, but there was something fishy about it. And I wasn't just talking about the one behind Tim's ear.

Midnight in Wapping. Tim and I were hiding in the half shell of a house directly opposite the gate that led to the dock where *Penelope* was moored. We'd been there roughly six hours. And six hours had never been rougher. We hadn't been able to dry before we got dressed and our clothes were damp and itchy. We were frozen and exhausted. Nobody had so much as driven past for an hour and then it had only been a taxi on its way home. It was a pitch-black, moonless night. Even the stars hadn't bothered to show up. The only light came from a streetlamp a few yards away, a dull glow that reflected in the windows of the empty boat.

So what were we doing there, watching a deserted dock on a deserted river in a deserted part of town? I couldn't really answer that question myself. It was just that somewhere inside me I was sure that the dock was the key. I was determined to stick with it. Powers had been there once. He might come back. And the Fence might come with him.

"Nick . . . ?" Tim asked drowsily. I thought he had fallen asleep.

I was about to reply when it happened. It was so totally unexpected that for a moment I thought I must be imagining things. But Tim had seen it, too. His hand gripped my arm. A light had gone on. Inside the empty houseboat.

A moment later, a figure appeared, climbing over the deck. He had opened the cabin door from inside and was walking down toward us, toward the gate.

"Where did he come from?" I whispered.

"He must have swum," Tim said.

"But he isn't even wet."

"Another boat, then?"

"Did you hear anything?"

Tim shook his head. Meanwhile the figure had reached the gate and was opening it, turning the padlock with a heavy brass key. He was dressed in dark trousers and shirt. He looked up and down the road, checking that there was nobody in sight. Then he went back to the boat.

"It's impossible . . ." Tim hissed.

"Sssh!"

There was a soft rumbling and a truck appeared, its tires crunching on the gravel. For a moment I thought it was going to drive right past, but then it stopped and reversed, coming to a halt with its back only a foot or so from the gate. It was the sort of truck you see outside houses when people are moving. The back folded up like a venetian blind. Two men got out and moved toward *Penelope*.

The first man—the one in the dark clothes—had been joined by three more, each of them carrying a crate the size of a tea chest. They were walking out of the boat as if they had been there all evening. But I knew that wasn't the case. The boat had been empty when we explored it. It had never been out of our sight since. So where had the men come from—and for that matter, the crates?

And that was only the start. The five men must have made a dozen journeys to *Penelope* and each time they returned to the truck they were carrying something more. First there were some more crates. Then there was a rack of coats, a stereo system, another dozen crates, and finally two oil paintings, each of them bigger than the cabin they'd just come out of.

By now they'd managed to fill an entire truck from an empty boat. The two men got back inside and it drove off—only to be replaced by a second. Then the whole procedure began again. This time they carried three antique tables, six crates, two rolls of carpet, four life-size statues, and—to cap it all—a grand piano. The piano had to wait for a third truck to arrive. The way things were going I wouldn't have been surprised if a ninety-piece orchestra had followed.

"It's impossible," Tim muttered for a second time.

And I had to admit, he was right. It *was* impossible. You must have seen that trick magicians do on the stage. They show you an empty hat and then they pull out a rabbit. Well, imagine the same thing only with an elephant and you'll get the general idea.

The whole operation took an hour. At last the third truck moved away. The man in the dark clothes locked the gate and went back to the boat. The light went out and then everything was just as it had been before it started.

For a long time neither of us spoke. Then Tim broke the silence. "Nick," he said, "do you think you could have missed all that when you searched the boat?"

"Missed it?" I almost screamed. "You were there, too. The boat was empty. We'd have had to be blind to miss it. I mean . . . where do you think it all was? Under the licorice paper?"

I closed my eyes, trying to work it all out. *Penelope* . . . I'd realized there was something screwy about it from the very start. And now I remembered what it was. It hadn't rocked. The morning we'd arrived in Wapping, I'd seen it. The Thames water chopping and swelling but the boat standing fast. Like it wasn't actually floating.

And then I thought about Johnny Powers. I followed him when he'd "gone to *Penelope.*" I knew what he'd meant by that now. But he hadn't gone anywhere near the dock. So maybe . . .

"Let's move," I said.

"Where?"

I smiled at Tim. "Where do you think? To the Wapping subway station."

UNDERGROUND

The subway system had shut down for the night, but just for once luck was on our side. The station must have been being cleaned, as the door was open and the lights were on. Not that they were expecting anyone to break in. What was there to steal after all? A ticket machine?

Even so, we crept in as quietly as we could—in case there was someone around to stop us. At the last minute I managed to stop Tim from trying to buy a ticket and we headed for the stairs. Then it was back down the winding staircase and onto the platform where I had lost Powers the first time. The station was as silent as a tomb. The arched brickwork could have come straight from a cemetery. All it needed was a couple of coffins to complete the picture.

We walked to the end of the platform and gazed into the endless night of the tunnel. There would be no trains for at least five hours. I assumed that meant there would be no electricity in the tracks either. If I was wrong, I might be in for a nasty shock in more ways than one. But I had to be right. The tunnel stretched underneath the Thames. Somewhere there had to be another passageway leading to . . . But I still had no idea what I'd find at the other end.

"Nick," Tim whispered. "I don't think there's going to be another train tonight."

"Tim!" I thought I'd explained it to him already. "We're not taking a train."

"Well, if you're hoping for a bus—"

"We're walking!"

"Down there?" Tim stared at me, his mouth as wide as the tunnel's.

"It'll be easy."

That was when the lights went out. The darkness hit us, a right hook between the eyes. There must have been somebody in the station after all because a moment later I heard the clatter of the iron gate being drawn across the entrance. Then there was nothing. No sound. No light. You had to pinch yourself to be sure you were still alive.

"Easy?" Tim's voice quavered out of the darkness.

"Hang on a moment . . ."

Fortunately I still knew what direction I was facing. In the total blackness I could have taken three steps and hurled myself off the edge of the platform. I reached out and found the wall. Then slowly I shuffled toward the tunnel. There were three steps leading down—I remembered them from my first visit. My foot found the top one and I lowered myself. My shoulder hit one of the fire buckets with a dull clang.

"Who is it?" Tim squeaked.

I ignored him. Somehow I found the sliding door. With

a sigh of relief I felt it open. I ran my hand up and down the wall, searching for the light switch. I hit it with my thumb. The light went on.

Tim came down and gazed into the storage room. It was just as I remembered it: telephones, dust, litter, and a tap. "There's nothing here," I said. "Let's go before something horrible happens."

"Wait a minute." Tim pushed past me.

"What's up?"

"I'm thirsty."

What happened next was the second big surprise of the night. Surprise? You could have knocked me sideways—in fact, Tim did knock me over sideways in his hurry to get out.

He'd gone over to the tap. He turned it on. Nothing came out. He muttered something and hit it with the heel of his hand. The tap swiveled in the wall. There was a loud click. And a moment later a whole section of the wall swung open to reveal a jagged entrance and a stairway leading down. I stared at it.

"Tim!" I exclaimed. "You've found it!"

"That's right!" he agreed. "I have!" He frowned. "What have I found?"

"The answer. That's how Johnny Powers disappeared the day I followed him. He didn't go into the tunnel. He went down there."

Tim looked at the stairs. "A secret passage . . ."

"And you opened it when you twisted the tap. You're brilliant!"

Tim smiled. "Just leave it to me, kid," he drawled. "I told you I'd look after you."

There were three flashlights hanging on the wall on the other side of the door. I took one of them and flicked it on. "Come on, then," I said.

"We're not going in, are we?"

"Of course we are! Don't you want to see where this leads?"

"No!"

We went in.

There must have been some sort of pressure switch built into the staircase because after a few steps the door swung shut behind us. I was glad in a way. Tim would probably have turned back given half a chance. And the way I was feeling right then I'd have probably taken the other half and followed him.

Led on by the beam of the flashlight, we went down. And down. The stairs, which had been narrow to begin with, got narrower. It was like being on the inside of a tube of toothpaste. The farther down we went the more buckled and bent the walls became. I could feel them pressing in on me. I just wondered what we'd find when we got squeezed out the other end.

The air was damp now. It smelled of the river. But there

was light ahead, a strange blue glow framed by a stone archway. I flicked off the flashlight and turned around to warn
Tim to keep quiet. I was half a second too late. Suddenly
there was a muffled explosion. It was so loud that for a moment I thought the bomb in the backpack had gone off. I felt
for my shoulders. They were still attached to my arms. Then
I realized. It was Tim. He had sneezed.

"Tim!" I hissed.

"I'b sorry," he whispered. "I thig I'b caught a cold."

"Well, try and keep it quiet."

"Sure, Nig."

We reached the bottom of the staircase and passed
through the archway. If the steps had looked like they'd been
carved out by some nineteenth-century smuggler, the corridor that now faced us was brand-new, white-tiled, with neon
strips burning at half strength in the ceiling. The floor was
raw concrete. I was about to move forward when a door
opened at the far end. Grabbing Tim, I ducked back behind
the arch.

"What is it, Johnny?" I heard a voice ask.

"I thought I heard someone, Ma," Johnny answered.

"What?"

"I don't know. Somebody sneezed . . ."

"It was nothing, Johnny boy. Ya're imagining things."

"Ya think so, Ma?"

"Sure, Johnny. Come and finish ya hot chocolate and gin."

The door closed and we breathed again. But at least I knew

now that Johnny Powers and his mother were here. The door at the end of the corridor had to lead to some sort of living quarters. It was just as well we hadn't wandered in or we'd have probably ended up in quarters and certainly not living.

A second corridor led off to the right. We took it. It stretched for about a hundred feet, the blue neon throwing blue shadows ahead of us. The underground complex was bizarre—a bit like a hospital, or a bit like the subway station it was directly under. There were no windows, of course. I could hear a faint hum in the air, some sort of ventilation system. How far did the complex reach? And how complex was it? It was impossible to say.

And "impossible" was the only word to describe what we found at the end of the corridor. I'd known it was large, but this was something else. In fact, it was so far beyond belief that I couldn't have imagined it in my wildest dreams, and I can tell you now, some of my dreams have been pretty wild.

The white tiles had ended. Forget the hospital. Forget the subway station. What we were looking at was a crazy museum, a vast chamber with archways running down both sides and classical pillars supporting a curving brick roof. It was an Aladdin's cave, a fantastic warehouse. It had to be the central depot. The place where the Fence kept his hoard.

Paintings lined the walls, some hanging, some leaning against the brickwork. Antique statues stood in a cluster, chandeliers hung from the archways. Oriental masks and mosaics poked out behind the pillars. Plain wooden crates spilled out gold and silver jewelry. We passed a mountain of video recorders and stereo equipment. We saw enough fur coats to wipe out a generation of minks, enough cutlery to equip a chain of hotels. You could have burgled every house in London, robbed every store, and stripped every museum and you still wouldn't have as much stuff as we saw there.

We'd found what we were looking for. As far as I was concerned, that was it. Now we could go to the police and give them everything they wanted . . . the Fence, Powers, and the proceeds from just about every robbery in the last ten years. All we had to do was get out again. It was as simple as that.

But of course nothing in my life is simple. And when things look easy, that's just when the problems begin.

My problems began with Tim. We'd gotten about halfway through the cavern when he suddenly uttered a strangled gasp. I thought he was going to sneeze again, but then he snatched something off a table and held it up to the light. When he turned around he was holding a vase, twelve inches high, bright blue, with some sort of bird painted on the side.

"I've foud it!" he whispered, his voice on the edge of a giggle. "I've agdually foud it!"

"Found what?" I asked.

"The Purble Peagog." He tried to clear his nose.

"Peagog . . ."

"Peacock?"

"You remember! The Ming . . ."

And it was. The Ming vase stolen from the British Museum had somehow found its way to the Fence and there it was, waiting to be sold. I didn't know what to say. Tim was grinning like a kid with a new toy. For the first time in his career he had actually succeeded. But this was no time for congratulations.

"Put your hands up!" somebody said.

I spun around. Nails Nathan was standing there. In the blue light his acne looked like the surface of the moon. But it was his hand, not his face, that caught my eye. It was holding a gun. And the gun was pointing at me.

"Nails . . ." I muttered, showing him my palms. "Maybe we can do a deal."

"No deal, Diamond," he snarled. "You're dead meat."

He was right. And Tim was the vegetable that went with it. It was all his fault. Johnny Powers had heard him sneeze. His mother hadn't been so sure, but Powers hadn't been taking any chances. He'd sent Nails out to investigate. And Tim and his wretched Ming vase had drawn him to us.

I looked around out of the corner of my eye, hoping for a gold-plated poker or anything I could hit him with. But there was nothing. Anyway Nails had me pinned down. He'd have blasted me before I could so much as blink. All he had to do was call out for Johnny and we'd be finished.

Then Tim sneezed a second time. It was so unexpected and so loud that Nails jerked around before he knew what he was doing. At the same time I was on him.

With one hand I grabbed his throat. With the other I went

for the gun. And that's how we stayed for a few seconds, like mad dancers doing the tango. He was trying to shout out, but I had a firm grip on his windpipe and no wind was getting through. I spun him around. Now I was facing Tim, who was still standing there, clutching his precious Ming.

"Hit him, Tim!" I hissed.

Nails was bigger than me and I could feel him getting away. There were only a few seconds left. The gun swayed between us as he tried to force it down toward me. I pushed with all my strength and it swung up again.

"Hit him!" I hissed again. "Use the vase!"

Tim moved forward. He was holding the vase in both hands and now he lifted it up, holding it above Nails's head. I waited for it to come shattering down. But Tim didn't do it. His arms were shaking. His face was a torment as he struggled with himself.

"I can't do it!" he muttered. "I can't do it, Nig."

Then the gun went off.

The bullet went so close to my face that I felt the heat against my cheek. It must have missed by a fraction, firing past my head and smashing a mirror on a wall behind me. The explosion was deafening. The underground warehouse amplified the smallest sound and the bullet and the shattering glass must have been heard in the next county.

I knew then that it was hopeless. With the echo of the gunshot still pounding in my head, I heard doors opening, footsteps running, voices calling out. Nails broke free. Once again the gun was aimed at me. I didn't move. Another dozen guns had joined it.

They had come from all directions, men that I had never seen before unless I had glimpsed them in the darkness of the dock. They were all dressed. Perhaps they slept with their clothes on. Perhaps they never slept. But now they were surrounding me. Nails rubbed his throat. There was murder in his eyes. I didn't need to ask to know whose murder he had in mind.

"I'm sorry, Nig," Tim whimpered. "I couldn't . . . not the Purble Peagog."

"Terrific, Tim," I muttered. "Maybe they'll use it to put your ashes in."

It wasn't a very nice thing to say. But I wasn't in a very nice mood. Tim gazed into the vase and put it back on the table. The circle of men separated. Johnny Powers and his mother had appeared. They were both in bathrobes. Ma Powers had curlers in her hair. I almost wanted to laugh. But somehow I guessed that if I did it would be the last sound I'd ever make.

"So ya came after me!" Powers snarled. "Ya rotten, stinking, two-timing rat."

"You seem to have changed your mind about me," I muttered.

"Sure I've changed. I thought ya was my friend. And all the time ya was working for the cops." Powers was quivering with anger. His face was white. But the madness was burning in his eyes. "I hate cops," he went on. "If I had my way I'd kill ya now—both of ya. And I'd do it slow."

"Why don't ya?" Ma Powers demanded. She was some mother.

"Because the Fence will want to see him." Powers glanced at Nails. "You okay?" he asked.

"Sure, Johnny." Nails sounded far from okay. His voice seemed to have gotten trapped in the lower reaches of his throat. He coughed. "I found 'em with the vase."

"The vase?" Powers shook his head, dismissing it. "I want them tied up and locked up. The Fence will be here tomorrow. We'll finish them then."

Nails signaled and four men moved in on us. We didn't even try to struggle. We were frog-marched to the far end of the gallery. It ended with a narrow corridor that led past a bank of machinery, the ventilation unit, and the electrical controls. On the other side I caught sight of an iron grille with an empty space behind it, the sort of thing you might see in an underground parking garage. We arrived at a door. Nails opened it and we were pushed into a small room.

One of the men had produced some rope. I'd always thought Nails was high-strung but that was nothing compared to what we were five minutes later. Our ankles, our knees, our wrists, our arms . . . Nails didn't miss a muscle. We ended up sitting with our backs to the wall. And that was the way it looked like we were going to stay.

The men left and Powers came in. He looked at us with a thin smile of satisfaction. His eyes were still ugly.

"Johnny—" I began. I was going to remind him of our time together in Strangeday Hall, how we'd been good friends, how I'd saved his life. But it wouldn't have cut any ice with him. This guy had ice for blood.

"Save ya breath, Diamond," he cut in. "Ya're gonna need it when the Fence gets here."

"Who is the Fence?" I asked. It wasn't going to do me any good now but I still wanted to know.

"Ya'll find out soon enough." Powers grinned unpleasantly.

"It's quite an outfit you got here," I said.

Powers nodded. "Right now ya're sitting a hundred feet under the Thames. It's right above you."

"The Fence built this place?"

"No. Some guy called Brunel did a hundred years ago. Nobody knew about it except the Fence. There were two tunnels, ya see. This was the first one. Only it ran into problems. Something about the limestone. So he started again a bit higher up. The Fence found the old tunnel, had it adapted." He stopped and sneered at me. "But why am I wasting my breath telling ya all this? Ya'll hear it from the Fence tomorrow."

He leaned down and gripped my face with an iron hand. I could feel his fingers gouging into my cheeks.

"The Fence will deal with you real good," he whispered.

Then he laughed, a high-pitched, trembling laugh. "But maybe there'll be something left for me. I'm gonna make ya wish ya'd never heard of me, Diamond. After I've finished with ya, ya'll wish ya'd never been born."

He turned on his heels and strode out of the room. The door banged shut and I heard a key being turned and two bolts being drawn across. Then there was silence.

We were tied up, locked in, and on our own. But there was one thing nobody had noticed: my backpack had been torn off my shoulders and flung into the corner. Nobody had opened it.

And the bomb was still inside.

UNDERWATER

The last time I'd been tied up in a room, it had been with a magician's assistant named Lauren Bacardi. We'd spent a bit of time together and she'd shown me one or two tricks of the trade. I'm not saying I was any Houdini. But I had learned something. For example, when Nails and the others were tying me up this time around, I'd remembered to keep all my muscles flexed. Now that they'd gone, I relaxed them. It didn't do much good. But it gave me a little play.

There was also something else. I was more or less dry after my dip in the Thames, but it had left me with a sheen of oil or grease. Like I said, the water was dirty. Now I was grateful for it. My skin was still covered with a slippery coating that made it easier to slide underneath the ropes. Easier but not that easy. It was going to take time.

Tim hadn't said anything for a while. That suited me. I still blamed him for getting us into this mess, him and his sneezing and his precious vase. But looking at him, I couldn't help feeling sorry for him. He looked about as happy as a turkey on Christmas Eve.

"Don't worry," I said. "We'll soon be out of here." I tugged and felt one of the cords slide over my wrist. Now all

I had to do was get it over my hand without dislocating my thumb.

"How?" Tim sighed. He had been watching me struggle. "Eben if we weren't died up, there's still the door. Logged add boated. And thed there's a whole arby of grooks waiting for us on the other side. All arbed. It's useless. It's hobeless. It's the end."

"That's what I like to hear," I said. "Always the optimist . . ."

Even so, I had to admit that it looked as if he was right. Fifteen minutes of fighting with the ropes and the only thing that was doing any running in that room was Tim's nose.

But I struggled on. There was nothing else to do. Tim dozed off, huddled up against the wall. Time passed. I didn't know how much time. There was no clock, no window, just a single bulb burning through the night. Maybe it was an hour. Maybe it was more. But just as I was about to give up, my left hand came free. The skin was torn and I had more bruises than a peach in an all-night grocery store. But my fingers moved. I was on my way out.

After that things went more quickly. I freed my legs next and finally my right arm. When I stood up, I felt like I'd just come out of the spin-dryer. But I'd done it. I'd actually done it. That just left the locked and bolted door and the army of crooks.

For the first time I looked around the room. It was long and narrow, about the same size as my cell at Strangeday

Hall. There was a second door at the far end, which I'd taken for a closet. But opening it now, I found it led into a small corridor running a few yards at right angles to the room itself. It must have been a storage area or something. It stopped with another solid wall. There was no way out from there. But it gave me an idea. I knew what I had to do.

I woke Tim up and began to untie him. As I worked, I told him what I had in mind.

"Are you oud ob your mide?" he asked. His cold had gotten much worse. "Forged id! Just die be up agaid. I'll waid for the Fedze."

"No way," I replied. I wasn't quite sure what he said, but I hadn't liked the sound of it. "Whoever the Fence is, he's one person I don't want to meet." I remembered what Powers had told me. He hadn't given anything away. "Or she," I added.

"Budnig . . ."

"Budnig?"

"Bud, Nig . . . !"

"No arguments. Once the door's open we'll have to move fast. And we've got to go back up there." I jerked my thumb toward the ceiling.

"You're bad," Tim said.

"Bad? What have I done that's bad?" I demanded.

"Not bad. Bad! Starg raving bad."

Tim was free by now. I helped him to his feet and left him rubbing his wrists, his ankles, and his nose. Somehow he was managing to do all three at the same time. I retrieved the backpack and opened it. Tim stopped what he was doing when he saw the bomb. I don't know what astonished him more. My idea or the fact that I'd been carrying it around with me all day.

Mickey Mouse's hand was touching the number eleven. I eased it back a bit, then reached for the switch. That took a bit of doing, I can tell you. I couldn't be sure the bomb wouldn't go off the moment it was turned back on. But the only explosion was another sneeze from Tim. He really knew how to time them. I carried the bomb to the door and left it there.

"You're bad," Tim said again.

"It's the only way out," I insisted. "The blast will tear out the door. But the walls look solid enough. There shouldn't be too much damage."

"Whad about us?"

"We go in there."

There was the corridor. I took one last look at the bomb, hoping I wasn't making a terrible mistake. Johnny Powers had said we were underneath the Thames. If the ceiling collapsed, it would be interesting to see if we were crushed before we were drowned. Either was preferable to being shot or strangled when the Fence arrived. And anyway I was sure I was doing the right thing. The force of the blast would be carried outward. It would smash the door and perhaps shatter a few mirrors. Tim and I would escape in the confusion. The more I thought about it, the more I liked it. Only I was careful not to think about it too much.

We went to the end of the corridor and crouched beside the wall, waiting. That was the worst part. I thought I'd given us two minutes' grace. It felt like two hours.

"Tim . . ." I began. I wanted to tell him what a great brother he'd been, how I'd always admired him. It wasn't true. I just thought he'd like to hear it. But he couldn't hear anything. His fingers were jammed into his ears so tight that I figured they'd meet in the middle. His eyes were shut. "All right," I muttered. "Have it—" The bomb went off.

The noise was deafening. It wasn't just loud. It almost tore my ears off. A cloud of dust stampeded down the corridor, throwing me off my feet. It seemed to go on forever. The lights flickered, went out, then glowed faintly. As the echo faded out, I was aware of the clatter of falling masonry and—the last sound I wanted to hear—the splash of water. With the dust streaking my eyes and clogging up the back of my throat, I got back to my feet. I looked around for Tim. Somehow the explosion had managed to tear his shirt in half. Or maybe he'd done it himself.

"Let's go!" I yelled, although it came out as a muffled croak.

There was no need for silence now. Already I could hear people shouting in the distance. Nearer to us, the ventilation equipment seemed to have gone into overdrive, the cogs and fan wheels screaming and grinding. The lights flickered again. We staggered back down the corridor and into the cell, or what was left of it. The bomb hadn't just taken out the door.

It had demolished the entire wall. I looked up. There was a nasty crack in the ceiling, zigzagging across. Water was seeping through, a thin sheet that splattered onto the broken concrete floor. But even as I watched, the downpour became wider, faster. A brick fell, narrowly missing Tim. Clutching him, I edged forward.

Outside the cell, everything was as chaotic as I'd hoped. It was hard to tell where the dust ended and the smoke began. But the effect was the same. Stretch out your arm and you couldn't see your hand. Some of the machines had caught fire. Through the swirling smoke I saw a sudden eruption of brilliant sparks. The ventilation system shuddered, snapped, and fell silent. More sparks of electric white burst out, buzzing like miniature fireworks. There was a rush of crimson flame. Behind us, the water poured down faster than ever. As we stood there hesitating, it lapped our heels. Water behind, fire ahead, smoke everywhere. Mickey Mouse had gone out like a lion.

I knew where I wanted to head while I still had a head to get there: through the gate that looked like the entrance to a parking garage. It was directly ahead of us, but before I could stop him, Tim broke free and ran off to the right. The smoke swallowed him up.

"Tim!" I yelled.

"The Purple Peacock!" he shouted back. "I can't leave it!"

I couldn't believe what I was hearing. I'd gotten us out. We could still make it to the surface. All hell was breaking loose. And he was going after the wretched Ming vase! For a moment I was tempted to leave him to it. But I couldn't. He was my brother. I was responsible for him.

But if someone else didn't kill him first, I'd do it once we were out of this mess. I plunged into the smoke after him. At least the explosion seemed to have unblocked his nose!

The smoke was like a curtain. After a few steps it suddenly parted and I found myself back in the main gallery. Things weren't so bad on the other side. The bomb had managed to smash perhaps a million dollars' worth of priceless china and glass. Tentacles of water were already creeping past to claim the Persian rugs and carpets. But the place was still standing. And the lights were still on.

I just had time to see Tim disappear behind the column when someone appeared, holding a machine gun. It was Nails Nathan. He swung around and I dived to one side, crashing headlong into a harp that collapsed with a great zing. It was accompanied by a crackle of bullets that swept past just above my head. A Rembrandt self-portrait on the wall behind me looked down sadly with about eighteen extra eyes. Nails ran forward. Keeping my head down, I scrambled on, desperately searching for a weapon or for somewhere to hide—ideally both.

"Find him! Kill him! Kill both of them!"

It was Johnny Powers. He had appeared on the scene— and he wasn't happy. His voice was hysterical, like a kid who's lost his parents. The ventilation system wasn't the only thing that had cracked that night. I knew complete insanity when I heard it. And I was hearing it now.

Nails Nathan was almost on top of me when I found it. It must have been stolen from some fancy antique shop. A medieval crossbow complete with bolt. It wasn't quite the weapon I'd had in mind, but it would do. It had a sort of ratchet with a lever to arm it. I pulled it back, then loaded the bolt. Nails was moving more cautiously now. I crouched down behind a marble table, waiting to get him in my sights. Then suddenly there he was, looking up at me.

He brought the machine gun around. I squeezed the trigger. The crossbow jerked in my hands and to my dismay the bolt missed him by miles, shooting over his left shoulder. Nails smiled. The bolt hit a pillar and ricocheted upward. Nails glanced up and screamed. The bolt had severed the wire of a chandelier, a huge thing that must have come out of some palace. The chandelier plummeted down and Nails disappeared in an explosion of lightbulbs and glittering crystals.

But this was no time for self-congratulation. Johnny Powers was getting closer and now his mother was with him.

"You look out for yaself, Johnny boy," I heard her say.

"Don't ya worry, Ma," he replied. "I'm gonna find that lousy, dirty, double-crossing . . ." His words became incoherent.

Ducking down behind the columns, I ran through the gallery. I could see Johnny Powers now. He'd gotten dressed and was holding a gun. There were six men with him, fanning out to search the place. The others had run on to deal with the flames. Ma Powers hung back in her bathrobe and curlers.

Fortunately I found Tim before they did. He was standing with the Purple Peacock, gazing at it like he was in some posh department store and he was thinking of buying it. It was incredible. Didn't he realize that we were still trapped underground with an awful lot of very awful people out to kill us? There are times when I think that in his own way Tim is as mad as Johnny Powers. This was one of them.

"Tim!" I whispered. "Have you quite finished?"

"Sure, Nick." He clutched the vase to him. He was actually smiling. It meant that much to him, finding it.

"Then do you mind if we go?"

"Ya're not going anywhere!"

Powers was standing only a few feet away. He hadn't seen me, but he had seen Tim. And now he'd gotten both of us. The six armed men formed a semicircle around us. They were all holding guns. They looked like an execution squad. In fact, they were an execution squad.

"Ya're finished, Diamond," Powers snarled. His face was distorted with hatred. "I should've plugged ya when I had ya before. But this time I'm not making any more mistakes. I'm gonna do it now." He giggled. "And I'm gonna enjoy it."

He raised his weapon.

I knew it was the end. But I still didn't expect it to happen so quickly. And it wasn't the end that I'd expected.

First there was a gunshot. But it wasn't Johnny's gun. It

came from the end of the corridor. The gun was torn out of Johnny's hand, clattering on the floor. The six men wheeled around. My eyes followed them.

Chief Inspector Snape of Scotland Yard stood there. He was alive. He was armed. There were about twenty uniformed policemen with him.

"All right, Powers," he said. "Come on out with your hands up. I've got this place surrounded. You haven't got a chance."

Then the roof collapsed.

I suppose it had only been a matter of time. Powers had spoken of a problem in the building of the tunnel—the tunnel that was now the Fence's headquarters. Something to do with the limestone. Whatever it was, it had been a splinter that had just been waiting for an excuse to turn into a yawning chasm—and the explosion had been that excuse. The whole complex shook. Then about a ton of bricks and broken stone crashed down on Powers, burying him. I didn't see what happened to the six men, because a second later the Thames followed. All of it.

If I hadn't been standing to one side, I'd have been killed there and then. Even so I was hurled off my feet. The last thing I saw was Tim, clasping the Purple Peacock. Then I was swept away, carried in a torrent of racing, foaming water. Somebody screamed.

Another section of the ceiling smashed down. A column tottered and collapsed, plowing into a grand piano and re-

ducing it instantly to matchwood. Televisions and video
recorders surged past, spinning in the current. Everything
was spinning. The water was roaring in my ears.

I'm going to drown, I thought. This is it. Prepare to meet
your Maker. And don't forget to ask Him why you got such
a raw deal.

But then a hand grabbed me and pulled me up into the air.
It was Snape. He had formed a human chain with the other
policemen. It reached back to the metal grille, which was also
the way they'd come in. After the initial impact, the flow of
the water eased off. It was about six feet deep. The *Titanic*
must have looked a bit like this with furs and jewelry floating
in the icy water. Another column snapped in half, unable to
stand the pressure. More stonework cascaded down.

"Tim!" I shouted.

For there he was, swimming toward me with one hand.
It was incredible. He wasn't only alive. He still had the Purple Peacock. And despite everything—the explosions, the
falling masonry, the flood, it was still in one piece.

"This way, laddie," Snape said.

I was too exhausted to do anything for myself anymore. I
allowed Snape to pull me through the water. I still couldn't
believe he was alive. And how had he found me? But expla-
nations could wait until later.

Two more policemen took hold of me and a moment later
I found myself sitting on dry land. Then Tim was pulled out
to join me, still holding the Purple Peacock.

We were on a sort of wooden platform. It was behind the metal grille, which Snape now closed. All twenty policemen were there, along with Tim, Snape, and myself and you could still have found room for more. There were two buttons set in a box on the wall. One was red, the other green.

"This had better work," Snape muttered.

He pushed the green button.

There was a whir of machinery and the platform began to move, sliding upward into blackness. For thirty seconds I couldn't see anything, but I could feel my stomach sink. And now I knew, of course. It had reminded me of an underground parking garage. Because the platform was nothing less than a huge elevator.

At last it broke into the light of the early morning. I looked around, blinking. And then I wanted to laugh. We had traveled up a shaft, up through the water. And I knew where we were. I should have known all along.

We were inside the *Penelope*.

"All right, Snape," I said. "Spit it out. How come you're alive? How did you get here? What's been going on?"

I was sitting on a bench near the river, wrapped in a blanket and holding a tin mug of hot tea. The Purple Peacock was in a cardboard box beside me. It was eight o'clock in the morning and for once Wapping was a hive of activity. There were police cars everywhere. A mobile canteen had been set up, supplying tea and bacon sandwiches. There were also two ambulances. I was fine, but Tim was being treated for shock.

The banks of the Thames were lined with constables holding nets. They were more like fishermen than policemen. For the past hour all sorts of treasures had been floating to the surface to be caught and taken away for identification. And they weren't the only things to fall into the police net. Ma Powers had been arrested, trying to escape through the station, and now she was being bundled into a police van.

By the time she got out of jail, she'd be Great-grandma Powers, and do you know, I almost felt sorry for her? After all, she'd only been looking after her boy. Which was more than my mother had ever done for me.

Johnny Powers and Nails Nathan were never found. Maybe they both drowned, but I have a feeling they both got away. It's certainly true that later that day two Japanese tourists got knocked out at the Thames Barrier and woke up minus their clothes, cameras, air tickets, and credit cards. Maybe that was the two of them and maybe even now they're out there, continuing their life of crime in Tokyo. If so—I just hope they stay there.

But the worst of it was that it had all been for nothing. We hadn't gotten the Fence. He hadn't been in the underground complex at the time and it was unlikely now that he would show up. The whole area had been cordoned off. Crowds of journalists and television cameras were being held

back behind the barriers. The river police were patrolling the
Thames and helicopters buzzed overhead. The whole of London knew what had happened, was being told about it on the
morning news. By now, the Fence was probably miles away.

"Where do I start?" Snape asked.

"How about with the way you framed me?" I growled. He
might have saved my life a few minutes ago. But that didn't
even the score. If it hadn't been for him I'd have still been
happily at school—or at least, as happy as you can be when
you're in a dump like mine.

Snape wasn't even a little bit apologetic. "I had to frame
you," he said. "You wouldn't play along otherwise."

"But that's criminal!"

"No. That's police work. But don't worry, my old son. All
the charges against you will be dropped now. And I did my
best to look out for you. I was never far behind."

"Yeah. How come you showed up like that?" I sipped the
tea; it was warm and sweet. I wouldn't have used either word
to describe Snape.

"You were bugged," Snape explained. "I had you on radar
every minute of the day."

"Bugged? How?"

"In your shoes." Snape pointed. "Your prison shoes.
There's a powerful tracking device in each of the heels."

"So . . ." Suddenly it came to me. "That night on the railway tracks in Clapham. It was you who cut me free!"

Snape nodded. "That's right. I saw you snatched by Big Ed's gang. We followed you there. Once they'd left you on the tracks, I came looking for you. I helped you get out."

"Well, thanks for that . . ."

"It was the same thing tonight," Snape went on. "We homed in on you under the river and I guessed you'd found the Fence. After that we came in to get you."

"You took your time."

"We were waiting for the Fence."

"Yeah—well, it looks like the one who got away."

"Don't worry about him, laddie. We've smashed his operation. And one of the gang will talk. You'll see. We'll catch up with him eventually."

"Just so long as you don't need any more help from me." I finished the tea. It was the first hot drink I'd had in thirty-six hours. "So how come you weren't killed?" I asked. "I saw you . . . in the car."

"I was lucky. I was in the backseat. The door was ripped off and I was thrown clear just before the car blew. The driver managed to get out, too. Then we went back and got Boyle."

"He's dead?"

"No. He's in the hospital. Third-degree burns."

"You're breaking my heart, Snape," I said. "I'll send him some flowers."

"That's good of you, lad."

"Sure. Dandelions."

Perhaps I was being a bit hard. But think about it. I'd been framed, tried and sent to jail, menaced, chased, shot at, kidnapped, knocked out, tied to a railway track, almost blown up, menaced some more, tied up again, half drowned, exhausted—and all for two policemen who hadn't even caught their man anyway. It wasn't as if I'd been given any choice. And what was I going to get out of it all, except for extra homework once I got back to school?

"You won't do so badly," Snape assured me. "There'll be a reward from the insurance companies for some of the stuff that gets recovered. That should be worth a bit."

We sat in silence, watching the activity all around us. I yawned. I was dog-tired. All I wanted was a bed. I'd even settle for a kennel.

Then Tim strolled over to us. He'd been fixed up by the doctors. Someone had lent him a sweater. And he was looking in a lot better shape than me. In fact, he was quite his old self. Which is to say that as usual he was totally impossible.

"Hi, Nick!" he said, smiling.

"Are you okay, Tim?" I asked.

He grinned. "This has been my greatest case. It'll make me famous. The man who got Johnny Powers!"

"What about me?" I demanded.

"You helped, kid. Maybe I'll even share some of the reward with you. In fact, I'll forget that fiver you owe me." He tapped me gently on the shoulder. I felt like knocking him out. "The British Museum will pay me plenty for the return of the Purple Peacock," he went on. "By the way, where is it?"

He sat down as he spoke. But he was so wrapped up in himself that he wasn't looking what he was doing. I saw his backside come down fair and square on the cardboard box. The cardboard crumpled. There was a dull splintering from inside. The color drained out of Tim's face.

The Purple Peacock had been stolen in Camden. It had found its way to Wapping. It had survived an explosion and a flood. But it hadn't survived Tim.

He'd just sat on it.

FRENCH TRANSLATION

It ended exactly the way it had begun—with French on a hot afternoon.

C'était un dimanche matin et il faisait chaud. Antoine et Philippe étaient dans le champ. Leur père dormait dans une chaise longue. Quelqu'un les appelait de l'autre côté de la palissade. C'était leur grandmère.

"Voulez-vous jouer au football?" demanda-t-elle.

The exercise was written up on the blackboard and we were being made to translate it out loud. Palis would call out a name and some poor soul would have to stand up and stumble over the next sentence. You weren't allowed to sit down until you reached a period. Why do French translations have to be so stupid? You sweat your guts out turning them into English only to find they weren't worth it in the first place. Fortunately I'd done this one the night before. If my name was called, I could cope.

"Sington!"

"It was a . . . er . . . *dimanche* . . . Sunday morning and it made warm."

"It was hot, you stupid child!"

Two weeks had passed since our escape from *Penelope*. In the newspapers, the story had slipped from page-one headlines to page-two comment to a few column inches on page three. Anyway, the press had left out more than it had told. For a start, nobody mentioned Tim or me. Snape had seen to that with something called a D-notice. *D* for "don't!" He said it would be better for me if my name was kept out of things. And better for you, too, I thought. What would the British public make of the British police framing and blackmailing British schoolkids? I mean, it simply wasn't British.

"Sit down, Sington. Goodman!"

"Me, sir?"

"Yes you, Goodman."

"Antoine and Philippe were in the field, sir."

In the end I'd gotten a four-line mention in some of the nationals. They said that I'd been released from Strangeday Hall "in the light of new evidence." In other words, my name was cleared. Only Snape and the authorities were making sure that it wasn't a name you'd read about too much.

"Hopkins!"

"Their father was asleep in a garden chair."

"Exactement."

Of course, I'd been the center of attention once I'd got back to school. The headmaster had made a speech about me during assembly. Everyone had made a lot of jokes. But it's surprising how quickly people forget these things. After a few days everything was back to normal. Sure enough, there was extra homework. Enough to fill an extra home. But I wasn't the hero anymore. I wasn't sure that I ever had been.

Palis hadn't changed either. He was his old, sarcastic, ear-tweaking self. He had barely said a word to me since I'd gotten back. It was as if he wanted to forget the evening we had spent together. I hadn't mentioned his involvement, the way he had helped me. I guessed he preferred it that way. But he could at least have said he was glad to see me alive.

"Simple!"

He called my name now and I got to my feet. It was hot and stuffy in the classroom. The sun was dazzling me. It was hard to concentrate on the words. Somebody did something from the other side of the palisade?

I remembered. "Someone called them from the other side of the fence," I said.

"Yes. That is correct, Simple. Now Buckingham! The next sentence . . ."

I sat down again.

My head was throbbing and I could feel the sweat beading on my skin. For a moment I thought I was ill. But it was something else. The voices in the classroom had become a dull echo. I screwed up my eyes and tried to focus on the blackboard. I'd seen something, read something, that was horribly wrong. Or maybe just horrible.

The French words in Palis's spidery handwriting blurred,

then straightened out. I plucked out the sentence I had just translated.

Quelqu'un les appelait de l'autre côté de la palissade.

The fence! That was it. I'd just said the word myself. The fence—*la palissade.*

Palissade.

Palis.

No. It was insane—a coincidence. I glanced at the French teacher. He was talking to someone else, but his eyes were fixed on me. And there was a cruel smile tugging at his lips.

And then suddenly it all made sense. Palis was the Fence. It couldn't have been anyone else.

When Snape had first come to visit me, he had told me that the Fence could be hiding behind an ordinary occupation—a banker or a shopkeeper, for example. He could also have been a teacher. In fact, with their afternoons off and long vacations, what better cover could there have been? And Snape had probably suspected him from the start.

The thought hit me like a bucket of ice. Why else would he have chosen me of all people to do his dirty work? He'd guessed that Powers would break out of Strangeday Hall. He'd hoped that I'd go with him. That was why he'd been there so coincidentally the night of the escape. I would recognize the Fence when I saw him. And if the recognition killed me, it would only prove that Snape had been right all along.

Palis . . .

Piece by piece it all fit together. Right at the start, in Woburn Abbey, I had been surprised by how much the French teacher had known about art and antiques. But of course, as the Fence, that had been his profession.

Then there was his flat—the expensive flat in Chelsea. I'd wondered how he could afford it. And the paintings! I'd seen what I'd assumed to be copies of Picassos on the wall. But I'd been wrong. They were the real thing!

I'd blown it from the moment I walked in there. Palis had rescued me from the police because he thought I was on his side. And once I was in the flat he'd been about to tell me everything.

Thank you for rescuing me . . .

Well, I had a good reason . . .

He'd been about to tell me that he was the Fence, but before he could speak I had ruined everything. I had told him I was working for the police and had sealed my own fate.

No wonder he'd been in a hurry to leave Wapping the next morning. He'd known about the bomb because he'd telephoned Powers the night before. I'd even heard the tinkle of the bell in my dreams. Poor old Tim had been dragged out of his bed on my account. Palis had cold-bloodedly arranged it all. He'd driven me there knowing that it was the last journey I'd ever make . . . at least, in one piece.

Palis . . .

The thud of closing books and the slamming of desks

brought me back to the present. I glanced at the clock. It was three-thirty, the end of the last lesson. Already people were running down the corridors as the school emptied.

What was Palis planning? Did he know that I knew? I looked at him carefully. There could be no doubt about it. He had handed me that sentence as a challenge. He was finished and he knew it. But he planned to take me with him.

"That is all for today," he was saying now. "*Malheureusement* I will not be with you next week. In fact, I am taking a vacation . . . a long vacation. I will not be coming back."

There was a groan of disappointment from the class—fake, of course. Nobody would be really disappointed if he fell off a cliff.

"You can go now," he went on. "All except Simple." He dropped the three words like daggers.

My fingers tightened on the desk. Everyone else had gotten up and begun to shuffle out. Palis slid his hand into his jacket. It was a casual movement but I had no doubt what he was holding on the inside. What could I do? If I tried to make a break for the door now, he would start shooting—and he wouldn't be too fussy about who he hit. But once I was alone, I wouldn't have any chance at all. By the next day I'd be back in the newspapers again. In the obituaries.

There was just one chance. He had more or less told me that he was the Fence. He knew that I knew. But did he know that I knew that he knew that I knew? Work it out. It made sense to me.

I walked forward innocently and stood in front of his desk. A pile of exercise books were stacked between us. I rested my hands in front of them. There were only seven or eight people left in the classroom, grouped around the door.

"Is it about the French translation, sir?" I asked.

"No." He blinked at me, wondering if I was more stupid than he thought. That was what I wanted him to think.

"I did do all the extra work you gave me, sir," I went on.

"It's not about that."

I pretended to scratch my nose, using the cover to look out of the corner of my eye. The doorway was clear.

"Mr. Palis . . . ?" I said.

At the same moment I jerked both my hands upward. He was already pulling out the gun but I'd taken him by surprise. The books flew into his face, knocking him off balance. At the same time I ran for it. I'd reached the door before he'd recovered. Even so, there was a sudden crack and the frame splintered as I passed through.

I was out. But I wasn't away.

Palis had a gun equipped with a silencer. Nobody had heard the first shot. Nobody knew anything was wrong. I looked left and right. The main entrance was blocked by a crowd of people, milling out into the yard. I went the other way, skidding along the corridor and crashing into a fire extinguisher. The second shot hit the extinguisher with a loud clang. I spun around a corner, colliding with Mr. Roberts as he came out of one of the classrooms.

"Simple . . . !" he began.

Palis fired again. The bullet drilled through six volumes of the *Oxford Medieval History* and buried itself in Mr. Roberts's shoulder. He screamed and passed out. I jumped over him and ran.

I came to a staircase and took the steps three at a time. I'd reached the first floor when a photograph of an old school cricket team seemed to blow itself off the wall just above my shoulder. With a fresh burst of speed I carried on to the second floor and then to the third.

Even as I went I was asking myself one question. Where was Snape? If he suspected Palis, he had to be somewhere near. It almost seemed as if the chief inspector wanted me dead as much as the Fence did.

The top floor of the school was given over to the biology and physics laboratories. The classes must have finished earlier because the rooms were empty now. There was no way out from here and no witnesses. Palis knew that. He was moving more slowly, his feet heavy on the stairs. I tiptoed through a pair of swing doors and into the biology lab, hoping he would miss me. A dissected rat stared at me from a glass case. A skull grinned beside a Bunsen burner.

Palis found me. There was another muffled cough and the skull disintegrated as his bullet hit it right between the eye sockets. I threw myself behind a counter. The Fence walked into the room.

Fortunately the blinds had been drawn in the room and

there wasn't much light. I crouched behind the bench, moving forward on my haunches. The bench stretched almost the whole length of the room. As I went one way, Palis walked the other. I could hear his footsteps but I couldn't see him. I didn't dare to look.

There were shelves under the bench, close to the floor. Each one was lined with bottles, filled with liquid of different colors. I took one and pulled out the stopper. The smell made my eyes water.

Palis stopped. He was breathing deeply. I reckoned he was only a few feet away, standing on the other side of the bench. I straightened up. And there he was, right in front of me. He fired.

I threw the bottle.

His bullet hit me in the arm, spinning me into the wall. My bottle hit him in the face, splashing its contents all over him. He screamed and rammed his hands into his eyes. A wisp of smoke curled out from underneath them. Pressing my own wound with one hand, I staggered out of the laboratory.

Another door stood open opposite. Still clutching my arm, I ran through it and up another flight of stairs. I didn't know where I was anymore. I just wanted to put as much distance between myself and Palis as I could. God knows what I'd done to his eyes. What had been inside the bottle? Sulfuric acid? Nasty . . .

The stairway led onto the roof. That was as far as I could go. It was a flat area no bigger than a tennis court with a

forty-foot drop on each side. But at least there was one good thing: I could hear the police sirens. I looked down and saw the first cars racing up to the school. There were still a lot of people around and now they were joined by a squadron of armed policemen diving out of the cars and taking up their positions around the building. As usual, Snape was late. But at least he had arrived.

"Simple . . ."

Palis was standing in the doorway, trying to hold the gun steady. He was a mess. White burn marks streaked one side of his face. One eye was closed. The other was bloodshot and staring. Half his hair seemed to have dissolved.

"You destroyed everything," Palis hissed. "My whole operation . . . my life's work."

"And now you're finished, Fence," I said. "This is your last post."

"*Oui.* But I'll take you with me, Simple. At least I'll have the satisfaction of that."

He squeezed the trigger.

But nothing happened. He had already fired six bullets. He didn't have a seventh.

Mad with rage, Palis screamed out and charged. He came at me like a wild bull. I stepped aside. Unable to stop himself, he shot over the edge of the building. Still screaming, he plummeted down. Then the screams stopped.

I walked back to the edge and looked down. It wasn't a pretty sight.

The Fence had impaled himself on a fence.

Ten minutes later I walked out of the school, my right arm hanging limp, blood spreading through my shirt. They'd wanted to carry me on a stretcher but I'd refused. I wanted to be on my own two feet.

From Woburn Abbey to Strangeday Hall to this . . . it hadn't been a lot of laughs. But I was alive. I was more or less in one piece. And that was all that mattered. Because life isn't so bad if you don't let it get you down, and although I had plenty to complain about, I meant to go on and enjoy it and save the tears for another day.

Turn the page for a preview of

THE FALCON'S MALTESER

a Diamond Brothers Mystery

THE PACKAGE

There's not much call for private detectives in Fulham.

The day it all started was a bad one. Business was so slack it was falling down all around us. The gas had been disconnected that morning, one of the coldest mornings for twenty years, and it could only be a matter of time before the electricity followed. We'd run out of food and the people in the supermarket downstairs had all fallen down laughing when I suggested credit. We had just $2.37 and about three teaspoons of instant coffee to last us the weekend. The wallpaper was peeling, the carpets were fraying, and the curtains . . . well, whichever way you looked at it, it was curtains for us. Even the cockroaches were walking out.

I was just wondering whether the time hadn't finally come to do something constructive—like packing my bags and going back to Mum—when the door opened and the dwarf walked in.

Okay—maybe you're not supposed to call them dwarfs these days. Vertically challenged . . . that's what it says in the book. But not this book. The truth is, this guy was as challenged as they come. I was only thirteen but already I had six inches on him, and the way he looked at me with cold, unforgiving eyes—he knew it and wasn't going to forget it.

He was in his midforties, I guessed. It was hard to say with someone that size. A short, dark stranger with brown eyes and a snub nose. He was wearing a three-piece suit, only the pieces all belonged to different suits like he'd gotten dressed in a hurry. His socks didn't match either. A neat mustache crowned his upper lip and his black hair was slicked back with oil. A spotted bow tie and a flashy gold ring completed the picture. It was a weird picture.

"Do come in, Mr. . . ." my brother began.

"Naples," the dwarf, who already was in, said. His name might have come out of Italy, but he spoke with a South American accent. "Johnny Naples. You are Tim Diamond?"

"That's me," my brother lied. His real name was Herbert Timothy Simple, but he called himself Tim Diamond. He thought it suited his image. "And what can I do for you, Mr. Venice?"

"Naples," the dwarf corrected him. He climbed onto a chair and sat down opposite my brother. His nose just reached the level of the desk. Herbert slid a paperweight out of the way to give his new client a clear view. The dwarf was about to speak when he paused and the nose turned toward me. "Who is he?" he demanded, the two *h*s scratching at the back of his throat.

"Him?" Herbert smiled. "He's just my kid brother. Don't worry about him, Mr. Navels. Just tell me how I can help you."

Naples laid a carefully manicured hand on the desk. His

initials—JN—were cut into a gleaming ring. There was so much gold around that third finger he could have added his name and address, too. "I want to deposit something with you," he said.

"Deposit?" Herbert repeated quite unnecessarily. The dwarf might have had a thick accent, but it certainly wasn't as thick as my brother. "You mean . . . like in a bank?" he continued, brilliantly.

The dwarf raised his eyes to the ceiling, took in the crack in the plaster, and then, with a sigh, lowered them onto Herbert. "I want to leave a package with you," he said briskly. "It's important you look after it. But you must not open it. Just keep it here and keep it safe."

"For how long?"

Now the dwarf's eyes darted across to the window. He swallowed hard and loosened his bow tie. I could see that he was scared of something or somebody in the street outside. Either that or he had a fear of storm windows.

"I don't know," he replied. "About a week maybe. I'll come back and collect it . . . when I can. You give it to nobody else except for me. You understand?"

Naples pulled out a packet of Turkish cigarettes and lit one. The smoke curled upward, a lurid blue in the chill morning air. My brother flicked a piece of chewing gum toward his mouth. It missed and disappeared over his shoulder.

"What's in the package?" he asked.

"That's my business," the dwarf said.

"Okay. Let's talk about my business, then." Herbert treated his client to one of his "don't mess with me" smiles. It made him look about as menacing as a cow with a stomachache. "I'm not cheap," he went on. "If you want a cheap private eye, try looking in the cemetery. You want me to look after your package? It'll cost you."

The dwarf reached into his jacket pocket and pulled out the first good thing I'd seen that week: fifty portraits of Alexander Hamilton, each one printed in green. In other words, a bundle of ten-dollar bills, brand-new and crisp. "There's five hundred dollars here," he said.

"Five hundred?" Herbert squeaked.

"There will be another five hundred when I return and pick up the package. I take it that is sufficient?"

My brother nodded his head, an insane grin on his face. Put him in the back of a car and who'd need a bobbing-head doll ?

"Good." The dwarf stubbed out his half-smoked cigarette and slid off the chair. Then he removed a plain brown envelope from another pocket. It was quite thick with something vaguely rectangular bulging in the center. It rattled faintly as he put it on the desk. "Here is the package," he said. "Once again, look after it, Mr. Diamond. With your life. And whatever you do, don't open it."

"You can trust me, Mr. Nipples," my brother muttered. "Your package is in safe hands." He waved one of the safe hands to illustrate the point, sending a mug of coffee flying.

"What happens if I need to get in touch with you?" he asked as an afterthought.

"You don't," Naples snapped. "I get in touch with you."

"Well, there's no need to be touchy," Herbert said.

It was then that a car in the street backfired. The dwarf seemed to evaporate. One moment he was standing beside the desk. The next he was crouching beneath it, one hand inside his jacket. And somehow I knew that his finger wasn't wrapped round another bundle of money. For about thirty seconds nobody moved. Then Naples slid across to the window, standing to one side so that he could look out without being seen. He had to stand on tiptoe to do it, his hands perched on the sill, the side of his face pressed against the glass. When he turned around, he left a damp circle on the window. Hair oil and sweat.

"I'll see you again in a week," he said. He made for the door as fast as his legs could carry him. With his legs, that wasn't too fast. "Look after that package with your life, Mr. Diamond," he repeated. "And I mean . . . your life."

And then he was gone.

My brother was jubilant. "Five hundred bucks just for looking after an envelope," he crowed. "This is my lucky day. This is the best thing that's happened to me this year." He glanced at the package. "I wonder what's in it?" he murmured. "Still, that shouldn't worry us. As far as we're concerned, there's no problem."

That's what Herbert thought. But right from the start I

wasn't so sure. I mean, five hundred dollars is five hundred dollars, and when you're throwing that sort of money around, there's got to be a good reason. And I remembered the dwarf's face when the car backfired. He may have been a small guy, but he seemed to be expecting big trouble.

Just how big I was to find out soon enough.